# Sherlock Holmes & THE MARK OF THE BEAST

".  .  . a precipitous ascent .  .  ."

# Sherlock Holmes & THE MARK OF THE BEAST

## from the Annals of John H. Watson, M.D.

Ronald C. Weyman

 Simon & Pierre

Toronto, Ontario, Canada

*We would like to express our gratitude to the Canada Council and the Ontario Arts Council for their support.*

*Marian M. Wilson, Publisher*

Illustrations: BBC Hulton Picture Library, London, 40, 50, 112; *Canadian Illustrated News*, p. 96; *Illustrated London News*, cover, 24; Mansell Collection, London, 32;  National Archives of Canada, 70, 96; Nautilus Memorial Submarine Force Library and Museum, Groton, Connecticut, 102; Nova Scotia Information Service, 128; Ontario Archives, 76.

ISBN 0-88924-219-4

1 2 3 4 5 • 93 92 91 90 89

**Canadian Cataloguing in Publication Data**

      Weyman, Ronald C., 1915-
          Sherlock Holmes and the Mark of the Beast

      ISBN 0-88924-219-4

I. Title.

PS8595.E85S5  1989    C813'.54    C89-090541-X
PR9199.3.W48S5  1989

**Design:** Christopher W. Sears

**General Editor:** Marian M. Wilson

**Assistant Editor:** Peter Goodchild

**Editor:** Christopher Redmond

**Printer:** Imprimerie Gagné Ltée

Printed and Bound in Canada

**Order from**
Simon & Pierre Publishing Company Limited/
Les Éditions Simon & Pierre Ltée.
P.O. Box 280 Adelaide Street Postal Station
Toronto, Ontario, Canada M5C 2J4

# Table of Contents

| | | page |
|---|---|---|
| | Foreword | 7 |
| I | The Evil Tide | 9 |
| II | The Mark of the Beast | 15 |
| III | The Man with the Shattered Arm | 22 |
| IV | Suite A-13 | 31 |
| V | A Depression over Iceland | 38 |
| VI | Sherlock Holmes Makes Inquiries | 46 |
| VII | Death in the Grand Saloon | 54 |
| VIII | The Solution of the Pine Box | 61 |
| IX | The Musician in the Tavern | 68 |
| X | At the Sign of the Golden Dog | 77 |
| XI | A Telegram from Home | 85 |
| XII | The Tides of Spring | 90 |
| XIII | A Life Is in Danger | 99 |
| XIV | "What Are You Doing in My Ship?" | 108 |
| XV | The Frightful Affair in the Baie de Ha Ha | 115 |
| XVI | A Demonstration aboard the Yacht | 123 |

# Table of Illustrations

page

". . . a precipitous ascent . . . " 02

"The ship's whistle sounded . . ." 24

". . . I have a horror of gambling . . ." 32

"The night of the big storm . . ." 40

". . . a certain *naiveté* . . ." 50

". . . the Victoria Tubular Bridge . . ." 70

". . . a *calèche* . . ." 76

". . . at Quebec, for two hundred years, we have built fine ships to sail the world . . ." 92

". . . a man's life . . ." 96

". . . Holland . . . builds a submersible . . ." 102

". . . the royal yacht *Victoria and Albert* . . ." 112

". . . in the full bloom of arrogant young manhood . . ." 128

# Acknowledgments

With great respect to Sir Arthur Conan Doyle.
Thanks to Annie M., Jack M., and Rita A.,
Jenny and Vanna W.,
for their encouragement.

# Foreword

On the fourth of May, 1891, the noted criminal investigator Mr. Sherlock Holmes plunged to his death at the Falls of the Reichenbach, in the mountains of Switzerland. So, at least, the world was given to believe. But three years later Holmes turned up again in London, alive and well, and accounting for his disappearance with a tall story that has been the subject of much criticism and historical speculation ever since.

At a time when England needed him most, the skeptics have asked, why would the intensely patriotic Holmes have disappeared in such a singular fashion? Why would the Government (which must have known, through the detective's influential and well-placed brother Mycroft Holmes, that he was alive) not have appealed to him to return far sooner than the spring of 1894?

The explanation must be that the Reichenbach Falls affair was deliberately staged; that there was a reason for Sherlock Holmes to disappear from public view in 1891; that he was in fact working in cooperation with the authorities, on a matter of which the world has had, to date, no account.

A bundle of handwritten notes has recently been uncovered in Canada which, if they are authentic, throw much light on this puzzling matter. At first sight no more remarkable than the other documents found with them — land surveys, ancient mortgages and a few family letters — these papers were discovered in a battered tin trunk of the sort formerly used to keep British military officers' effects clean and dry. The trunk contained also a cigar box in which were several medals, identified by experts as dating from the Second Afghan War period of the early 1880's, and a pair of old silver-backed hairbrushes engraved with the initials "J. H. W."

These items were among the effects of one Jean Poirier of Montreal, who had received them in settlement of the reduced estate of his English grandfather. That gentleman, it seemed, had acquired land north of Montreal in the year 1892, before later moving to Essex County, New York. There is some reason to believe that the grandfather of Jean Poirier was a nephew of John H. Watson, M.D., of London — the same Dr. Watson who was the personal friend and historian of Sherlock Holmes.

The handwritten notes were spare, and at times illegible. It has therefore been necessary for me, in preparing the expanded version of them which appears in these pages, to employ the balance of probabilities and even, at times, conjecture. I have, however, tried to be faithful to their style, where that was possible, as well as to the facts which they present.

A puzzling question naturally arises: given the obvious importance of the affairs which this narrative describes, why were Watson's notes about it consigned to the dusty trunk rather than elaborated for publication in the *Strand* magazine like many of Holmes's other adventures? The obvious answer is that their very importance, together with the involvement of the Prince of Wales and other prominent persons, made it impolitic for the truth to be known until generations, not merely decades, had passed.

Further, however, we must recognize how unprecedented are the challenges put before Sherlock Holmes in this case. Watson, or his literary agent or his publisher, may have concluded that readers would not find this Holmes entirely familiar or congenial. In the affair which these new-found notes describe, Sherlock Holmes is presented as a diplomatic agent, a man of action, what would now be called an international secret agent. It may have been Dr. Watson's cautious view that the Victorian public would accept Holmes only as the avenger of wronged maidens and the scourge of villainous squires in their country houses. We are fortunate to live in an age which can take a broader view of this nineteenth-century titan.

*Ron Weyman*

Beaver Valley,
Ontario, 1989

# Chapter I
# The Evil Tide

Contrary to the hope and expectation of my late friend Mr. Sherlock Holmes, the death of his archenemy Professor Moriarty, for which he had been prepared to sacrifice his own life, did not put an end to crime in London. Whether or not Moriarty had in fact sat like an evil spider in the centre of a web of intrigue, directing every aspect of the great city's criminal activity, I cannot tell. Suffice it to say that the months which followed Moriarty's death, in May of the year 1891, shewed little change in London's deplorable round of robberies, murders, and other nefarious activities, and it was with a heavy heart that I saw the tentacles of crime reach from the vilest alleys up to the highest offices in the land, with my friend no longer alive to hold back the evil tide.

The long, hot summer of 1891 eventually passed, and the fogs of November once again swirled in the London streets. Street lamps were lighted by four o'clock in the afternoon, but did little to relieve the dreary aspect of the city. The figures of passing strangers loomed out of the yellow mist, muffled and cloaked against the cold, hats pulled down, dripping with moisture. Hansom cabs glided by, horses' hooves sounding hollow in the fog, the cabbies' wet mackintoshes gleaming dully under the fitful glimmer of the lamps.

From time to time, I found myself involuntarily peering into the startled face of a stranger, or following a dimly seen figure through the mist, as if in search of Holmes's familiar form, or of a fuller acceptance of his untimely end. London, the great city that Holmes had brought brilliantly alive for me, was without him drab and meaningless. It was a situation not to be borne, and I presently summoned the resolve to take up the reins of my own life again and to go abroad, away from the streets that every minute reminded me of my friend.

In my younger and more romantic days, I had worked for a time as a ship's surgeon on P. & O. vessels plying to India and Australia. In my urge to get away, I determined to enter this occupation again. But it was not until spring that my affairs were wound up, and I was offered a berth by the Cunard Shipping Line in their splendid steamship *Etruria*, offering passenger service between Liverpool and Canada.

It was with a feeling of relief that I finally signed the necessary papers, made various purchases, and took a cab back to my lodgings in Kensington. The cabby helped me in with my parcels, and civilly accepted sixpence for his labours, giving me an old soldier's salute on his way out.

As I hung my hat and coat in the entrance hall, I found myself humming a music-hall ditty. I was pleased, my mind at last resolved. I was looking forward to the comfort of my armchair, intending to review my plans over a glass of brandy and to enjoy the warmth of my fire, which I would soon be leaving far behind. I opened my study door and carried in my purchases, then paused and stopped humming. The room seemed inordinately dark. The shutters at the windows were closed. I moved to open them, but felt another presence in the room and stopped, frozen in the middle of my gesture.

An endless moment passed while I waited, ready for I knew not what. A cab rattled in the street. I moved again.

"Keep the shutters closed, Watson." It was undoubtedly Holmes's voice, low-pitched but clear and penetrating as always. Holmes!

Contrary to what I may have written elsewhere, I did not then faint, for either the first or the last time. I remember my one and only faint well enough; it was on the Afghan frontier when I was spent with loss of blood from Jezail bullet wounds. On this occasion I reacted only with stillness, even my breath ceasing for a moment as I realized the cruel deception Holmes had been playing upon me for six months and more.

"Watson, are you quite all right?"

"Of course I'm all right," I responded with some asperity. "Where the devil are you?"

"By the fireplace, in the dark, sitting in your easy chair."

"And drinking my brandy." That, I think, assured me, as much as the voice itself, that my visitor was indeed Sherlock Holmes. It seemed the final touch of arrogance.

There was a faint movement in the corner of the room, a creak from my leather armchair. The face of Sherlock Holmes emerged from the shadows. He peered at me, his familiar hawk-nose and hooded grey eyes sardonic in the flickering firelight.

"How do you know I am drinking your brandy?"

"How?" I replied. "Holmes, I can smell it."

"Of course." He surveyed me a moment longer, then retired again to the shadows. "Elementary, my dear Watson," he said, and my patience snapped altogether.

"Holmes, look here, what the devil have you doing?" I burst out.

He looked up at me from the comfort of my armchair, glass in hand, his face thinner and paler than I had remembered it.

"My dear fellow, I thought you'd be glad to see me." He sounded hurt.

"Glad?" I replied in a tone of anger. "Of course I'm glad. But dash it all, Holmes, you can't simply leap into that dreadful torrent at the Reichenbach Falls, locked in the arms of Moriarty in a confounded death struggle, and be written off and mourned as dead — then turn up here six months later as if nothing had happened. And drink my brandy!"

"You were worried about me." Holmes eyed me with amusement, but his voice was tolerant. "Watson, my dear fellow, you look as if you could do with a glass of something yourself."

"I could, as a matter of fact." I crossed to the sideboard and poured myself a stiff brandy, drinking half of it at a gulp. "May I put on a light, do you suppose?"

"Yes, of course."

I lit a gas jet, then went to the fireplace and poked the coals into renewed flame. Holmes watched me from the shadowed depths of the chair as I recovered my equanimity a little.

"You have caused some of us considerable anguish, you know," I told him. "It was in the papers. People went into mourning."

"What was I supposed to do?" Holmes's voice was calm and reasonable.

"But the Reichenbach Falls! Your death — staged, it would seem."

"The battle at the Falls was real enough, Watson," he said grimly. "And my deception was necessary. I had my escape route planned."

"What about Moriarty?"

"Moriarty perished in the dreadful chasm below the Falls. I am sure of it." His eyes gleamed in the firelight.

"May I ask, then, where you have been?"

"I spent some months in the South of France, in Montpellier. I have access to a laboratory there." He drained his glass and put it down empty, then took a well used pipe from his jacket pocket. "I was doing some research into coal tar derivatives." He paused. "And trinitrocellulose and castor oil."

"Castor oil? what on earth for?"

"Smokeless gunpowder," replied Holmes. He patted his pockets, and came up empty.

"I've kept some of your shag in a tin on the mantelpiece," I assured him.

He reached a long arm for the tobacco tin and filled his pipe. "Thoughtful of you, Watson."

"There's no such thing as smokeless gunpowder," I told him firmly, as befits a man who served actively on the Indian Frontier, there experiencing many a shot fired in anger. Not content with reappearing in this inconsiderate way, Holmes was assuming knowledge in a field of which he could know little.

"There is now," said Holmes quietly. "Reach me a light, would you, old fellow?"

I stooped over the fire and lit a spill for his pipe. Holmes accepted it with a grunt of thanks, and his head was soon wreathed in acrid clouds of his favourite tobacco. He relaxed more deeply into the armchair, and smiled at me.

"How long is your engagement for, Watson?" he asked conversationally. "A single voyage, or longer?"

"Good Lord!" I exclaimed. "Is nothing secret from you?"

"I'm sorry, my dear fellow. I cannot help putting two and two together." He blew out a cloud of smoke. "When I let myself in — you really should do something about that old-fashioned Reilly door lock, by the way — I noticed an old steamer trunk put out, newly dusted. Entering your study, I see on your bookshelves empty spaces where books should be. Where are they? Aha! I see them on the table beside the door. Specialized medical books. *Emergency Surgical Procedures While at Sea*, for instance. Neatly beside them is a travelling surgical kit in its scuffed leather case. A relic of earlier days, eh Watson? Old, but still serviceable."

"I might say the same of myself, Holmes. Old but still serviceable."

"Then you enter, carrying parcels wrapped in stout brown paper and tied neatly with sisal. They appear newly purchased, and they bear the label of a prominent London haberdasher, Messrs. Gieves of Bond Street, supplier of officers' uniforms and gentlemen's frontier clothing. A moment ago, you were obliging enough to bend over the fire to provide me with a light for my pipe. I glimpsed a document displaying the rampant lion of the Cunard Shipping Company, not a passenger ticket but a contract of some sort. Conclusion: you are about to travel with Cunard, not as a passenger but, given your background, as ship's doctor."

"Is there any more, Holmes?" I asked patiently.

Holmes set down his pipe, and put the tips of his fingers together. Leaning back in the chair, he closed his eyes. "Where and when is Dr. Watson going in his new appointment as ship's surgeon? His state of readiness is suggestive of imminent action. When does the next Cunarder sail? The *Etruria*, modern, well appointed, sister ship to the *Umbria*, seven thousand, seven hundred tons, queen of the Atlantic, with a westward crossing in six days, two hours, twenty-seven minutes, departs from Liverpool

Wednesday next, bound for Quebec, making the first spring sailing to coincide with the ice moving out of the St. Lawrence River." Holmes opened his eyes and shot me a look. "You left a shipping list on the sideboard."

I felt like a schoolboy caught in a misdemeanour. "Quite correct, Holmes," I said.

He positively beamed at me. "Admirable," he replied.

"What do you mean Holmes, 'admirable'?"

"We shall be in the same boat."

In spite of myself I felt a quickening of my pulse. I had become used to his absence, and had determined to proceed with my own life. Now Holmes was back, without apology, taking over once more.

"I say, Watson," he began suddenly, "would you be good enough to glance through the shutters? Is there anyone outside, on the pavement? Any loiterers in the street?"

I turned my attention to the street. Daylight was falling, and shadows were filling the corners and doorways, but nothing moved. I turned back to Holmes and my mouth fell open with astonishment. In place of Holmes, there rose to his feet a shorter, stouter man whose bunched-up shoulders strained at the rough material of his jacket. A knotted sweat-rag adorned his throat, a broken peaked cap his head. He looked at me sideways, like a London cock-sparrow, a cheeky smile exposing a mouth notable for its lack of teeth. He lifted a grubby knuckle to his brow in a salute.

"Fanks, guv'nor, I 'ave to go nah." The gummy voice was pure Old Kent Road. I chuckled at the performance.

"Really Holmes, you're incorrigible."

The cheeky eyes abruptly hardened. As they met mine, piercing and intent, the laugh died in my throat.

"Watson, I must impress upon you, in utter confidence, the seriousness of the affair upon which I am now embarked."

"Holmes?"

"It would not be inaccurate to say that the balance of world power, indeed the future of the Empire, is at stake." Coming from the mouth of this costermonger, Holmes's words seemed bizarre in the extreme. They struck a chill into my heart. He came closer and spoke again, his voice quiet and deadly.

"At this very moment, there is being perfected, here in London, what its creator has described as 'a diabolical weapon before which nothing could live.' Whatever we do, Watson, or fail to do, this weapon *will* be perfected, and future generations will have to live with it — and die because of it." His voice was harsh.

"Holmes, that is appalling!" I cried.

"It *is* appalling." His eyes bored into mine.

"Yes?"

"Who, among the world powers, is to control such a weapon?"

I made no attempt to reply.

"That is the perilous question that besets Her Majesty's Government." He paused, gauging my response. "Watson, I have been asked to take a hand in the matter. The highest authority in the land will be awaiting my report. I shall need your help."

My heart leaped. "You have it," I replied without hesitation.

He looked at me a moment longer.

"Good," said Holmes, and he stepped back. His shoulders slumped, his head went to one side, the gap-toothed grin leered at me.

"I'm orf then, guv'nor. Don't bovver to see me aht."

In a moment my companion had gone, leaving only the smell of tobacco smoke, and an empty brandy glass, as evidence of his visit — of his return, as it seemed to me, from death.

# Chapter II
# The Mark of the Beast

The following day I had barely opened the *Telegraph* over a dish of bacon and eggs and a pot of Darjeeling breakfast tea when a smart landau, fresh horses pawing the pavement, drew up outside my Kensington lodgings. A brisk young fellow, top-hatted and morning-coated, sprang out of the vehicle, a creamy envelope in his hand. He glanced up, to confirm the number of my house I presumed, then vanished from my sight. In a moment the brass knocker on my front door sounded. Wiping the egg yolk from my chin I left my breakfast table to answer its brisk summons.

"Dr. Watson, sir?" The morning sun shone upon his fresh boyish face and side-lighted his carefully groomed side whiskers. He exuded a fresh scent of lavender.

"I am Dr. Watson."

"Compliments of Sir Henry, sir." He handed me the envelope. It was thick, creamy, embossed. "Would you be good enough to sign for it, sir?"

He smartly offered a receipt book and a fountain pen, which he uncapped for my use. The newfangled gadget promptly shot a blob of black ink onto his immaculate white cuff.

"Damn the jolly thing — excuse me, sir!" He dabbed at the mess with his handkerchief.

"Would a pencil do?" I said helpfully, pulling one from my breast pocket. Having signed for and accepted the envelope which came from Her Majesty's private secretary, I returned to my interrupted breakfast. With a clean butter knife I reverently slit open the thick paper and drew out a formal invitation to attend a Firework Display, graciously sponsored by Her Majesty. It was signed with a flourish in the name of "Sydney Home-Whitby, aide-de-camp." There was a pencilled addendum: "Bring your black bag and do try to look like an eminent Harley Street physician. A cab will pick you up in good time. S. H."

It was with great care, the following day, that I conducted my morning toilet, bathing, shaving, even — dare I admit it — rubbing a little pomade into my thinning hair. I made sure of fresh linen, a silk foulard tied with care, my best frock coat and silk hat. When my eye fell upon my medal ribbons — the few military decorations I had picked up in the Afghan war — I lifted them from the cigar box in which I kept them, placed them on my breast pocket, and surveyed myself in the mirror.

"Really Watson, you're still quite the dog!" I said aloud to my reflection. The royal invitation, however, did not mention "decorations," so I regretfully restored them to their box.

I heard the clatter of hooves in the street, and the grating of iron-shod wheels against the curb. For a royal occasion I suppose I had anticipated a coach-and-four, with two powdered footmen up behind, or at least a smart brougham with a liveried driver, but the conveyance which stood outside my door was an ordinary London cab, of no distinction whatever. The cabby remained in his seat.

"'Op in, guv'nor."

I swallowed my disappointment and climbed into the vehicle. We started off at a smart enough pace, but instead of heading towards Windsor as I had anticipated, the cab turned and took me in the other direction, deeper and deeper into London's East End and the dock district. Thoughts of Handel's *Royal Firework Music*, elegantly gowned and perfumed ladies, and the popping of champagne corks, all faded, to be replaced by the memory of Holmes's parting words. I felt an increasing sense of foreboding.

The cab swung from one grimy street to another, until somewhere in the vicinity of Woolwich we finally stopped. I could hear the hoot of a tug and the cry of sea gulls. The cabby peered down at me from his perch.

"'Addon 'All, guv'nor."

It was a low, ugly building, red brick under the grime of decades. Dirt lay in the gutter, and a discarded newspaper fluttered in a gust of wind from the river. The tide was out, for I could smell the stink of the exposed mud flats.

"Are you sure?" I asked.

"Quite sure, guv'nor."

"Right." I climbed out onto the street. "How much?"

"It's on the 'ouse," said the cabby. He clucked to his horse, turned and clopped off down the street.

The building sat squat and ugly before me. Small barred windows were set high in the walls, and shadowed under an archway was the front door, heavy and ironbound. As I moved towards it and found a bell pull, a gust from the river blew dust and dirty newspapers around my trouser legs. A steel shutter in the door slid open and a pair of bright blue eyes appeared. The instant I held up my invitation, the shutter snapped closed. There was the metallic sound of heavy bolts being withdrawn, and in a moment the great door swung silently open for me to enter.

The young man who stepped forward to greet me, alert from his sharp eyes to his highly polished half-Wellingtons, was trimly attired in the undress uniform of one of Her Majesty's Household Regiments.

"If you will come this way, sir, the demonstration is about to start."

He led the way along a passage and then down a wide stone staircase, the steps worn and the foundation walls scarred, from what causes or from how many years of use I could only surmise. Another massive door opened smoothly, and I found myself in a vast cavern of a room, its rock walls vanishing in shadow and distance. A smell of burnt gunpowder and cigar smoke took me back at once to the Indian frontier, to the shot and shell and loss of life in the fatal battle of Maiwand. Murray, my devoted orderly, was throwing my wounded body across a pack horse. In the carnage of the battlefield, he was smoking a Burmese cheroot.

I shook off the memory and surveyed the tunnel-like room before me. At some distance, perhaps four hundred yards away, acetylene torches flared overhead, casting an intense white light on what at first glance appeared to be human figures. Whether they were figures modelled in the round, or whether they were merely silhouettes, I could not tell at that distance. But they were uncanny in their realism, a crowd of twenty or thirty faceless passengers, who, under the flickering white light, appeared to dance gently together.

Closer to me, silhouetted against the flares, a group of top-hatted men of affairs waited in attitudes of patience, sitting or standing and smoking or conversing in low tones. Centred in the near end of the hall, a little removed from the group, a bulky shape rested on the stone floor. It was about the size and shape of a costermonger's barrow, shrouded in a canvas cover. I had the curious sensation that I was attending a funeral — whose funeral, I could not say.

"Dr. Watson! How good of you to come!" A figure detached itself from the group, and my observations were interrupted. "I am Sydney Home-Whitby, aide-de-camp."

I recognized Holmes in spite of the plummy hothouse accent, then becoming fashionable in Mayfair, which he had assumed; his dress and deportment, equally studied, were reminiscent of Beau Brummel of an earlier time.

"Look here, do come and meet one or two people. Hugh Farnbrough-Smyth from the War Office. Ronnie Harrison, fireworks expert *extraordinaire*." He took me over to the edge of the group. "Dr. Watson has had considerable experience with fireworks, on the Indian frontier, actually. First-hand knowledge, what?"

In shadow, apart from the group, three men were talking quietly. Watches were consulted and the three moved apart, one of them, an immense bear of a man, confronting the entire group. Heads turned in his direction. Deliberately, he dropped his half-smoked cigar on the stone floor, and ground it under his foot.

"Your Lordships, gentlemen. Ready or not, I am told we have to get on with this tea party." The voice was American, rumbling up from his deep chest. Other conversation ceased, and all eyes turned to the speaker, who surveyed his audience. His own eyes were cold and pale, shadowed by heavy black brows. A high, smooth forehead was topped by a shock of prematurely white hair. He was a big man, of commanding presence.

"My name is Hiram Maxim. I am an American, an inventor, and I'm here today to demonstrate to you a weapon of remarkable efficiency — one which will change the fortunes of the nation that possesses it."

There was a murmur in his audience, a thrill of anticipation: none amongst these aging politicians could resist the promise of renewed potency.

"Since the beginning of time, civilization has advanced, protected by increasingly sophisticated weapons," Maxim went on. "The big rock over the little rock. The iron sword over the bronze sword. Muskets over bows and arrows. The French *canon de feu* over the musket. In recent times the American Gatling gun, with ten revolving barrels — a clumsy and inefficient instrument, gentlemen, if I may say so, but a step forward."

Holmes was beside me on the fringe of the group. "This man fascinates me, Watson," he said close to my ear.

"He terrifies me," I whispered back.

"A fellow countryman of mine, Mr. Samuel Colt of Hartford, Connecticut, a few years back, invented a 're-vol-ver,' a big efficient handgun, gentlemen, four pounds in weight, a nine-inch barrel, six chambers, six rounds, cap and ball. Bang! Bang! Bang!" With his pointed forefinger, he made as if to fire into his august audience, some of whom flinched under his impetuous performance. "Back in the Sixties, we called it the Peacemaker. Gentlemen, that gun cleaned up the war with Mexico, it settled the Civil War, it subdued the Western Plains and changed the course of history."

Cigar smoke rose and caught the light from the acetylene flares. The top hats and broadcloth moved uneasily.

"Today, gentlemen, with Russia pushing at the gates of India, the Boers preparing to take over in South Africa, the Germans expanding their Navy, and every upstart European nation looking at the other guy's territory, I want to tell you that I am glad your good Queen Victoria, bless her, her generals and her ministers, some of whom are here today, see the handwriting on the wall. Yes-siree! The guy with the best is the one with the most! I am talking about *firepower*, gentlemen, and I will show it to you *now*!"

Again there was a murmur from his audience, a shifting of feet, a rustle of broadcloth, the flare of vestas as cigars were relit. Maxim held up his arms like an orchestra leader about to conduct Wagner in this frightful place. He waited a full half-minute for the group to become quiet again. Presently, when the only sound was that of the gas fizzing and sputtering in the flaming torches, Maxim's hands descended and the overture began. Two men sprang from the shadowed recesses of the stone wall and took up positions on either side of the shrouded shape that awaited our attention. They stood for a moment, then with one concerted action swept aside the canvas covering.

Revealed before us, squatting evilly on the stone floor, was a gun like none that I had ever seen previously. Instead of the clumsy multi-barrelled Gatling with which I was familiar, here was a sleek single-barrelled weapon mounted on a slender steel tripod, its polished surfaces glinting in the torchlight. Like a venomous snake looped through the gun's firing mechanism, a long steel-and-leather belt carried a lethal load of cartridges.

The top-hatted figures shifted and craned their necks to see the gleaming weapon more clearly.

"Your Lordships, gentlemen." Maxim spoke and his voice echoed from the stone walls. "You are looking at a weapon, a type of machine gun, never before seen on earth. It is fully automatic, capable of firing six hundred and sixty-six rounds a minute. It has a killing range of over two thousand yards, and it can lay down the most massive, the most effective firepower in human history." The torches behind him cast a nimbus of light around his white shock of hair.

"The mark of the beast," Holmes murmured in my ear.

"What?"

"Book of Revelation. Chapter 13. Look it up."

"Gentlemen, are there any questions?" said Maxim.

"Farnbrough-Smyth here, War Office. When you spoke to me earlier, you mentioned getting rid of the — uh — bugs. What did you mean by that?"

The massive head lifted. "I mean, sir, that with all due respect, I have been under pressure from your Government to move as quickly as possible."

"In plain English, sir, if you will?"

"Then, sir, in plain English, I was promised the support of your best craftsmen, machinists, gunsmiths and metal workers. I have not had that support. My complaints have fallen upon deaf ears, sir, in your department as well as others."

Members of the group shifted uneasily. A hurried consultation was taking place, *sotto voce*, between Farnbrough-Smyth and a stout, bearded gentleman. I heard Smyth say, "It was a matter of secrecy, sir," and the other reply, "Secrecy be damned! You are going to lose this man. He is going to slip away!"

Maxim was continuing to speak with force and persuasion. "There is also the matter of the powder. I need not remind the members — the military members, at least — of this august company, that black gunpowder is dirty stuff. It is okay for old-fashioned firearms, but not suitable for my machine gun. Every so often it fouls up the working parts and puts the gun out of action until it is stripped down, cleaned, and reassembled. I have repeatedly asked for chemists to assist me in developing a smokeless powder, a new and more efficient explosive, in fact."

I glanced at Holmes. His Mayfair affectations had quite vanished, and he sat very still, watching Hiram Maxim.

Again there was a hurried consultation, and again Farnbrough-Smyth spoke up. "Is there anything to be gained, then, at this time, by this proposed demonstration?"

"Indeed there is something to be gained! It will be demonstrated that we have one hell of a weapon here, and, given the right political support, one which will guarantee the future safety of your nation!"

"An alternative, sir, I suggest, is to delay the demonstration until such time — "

"An alternative, sir," exploded Maxim, "is to pack up the whole shebang, and return to America!"

"Burroughs here, Foreign Office. May I ask why it is that you, an American, are offering your invention to us here in Britain, rather than to your own country?"

"A fair question, sir. Suffice it to say that your British patent laws are more attractive to the inventor than either the American, German, or French. And I'm an inventor. Frankly, sir, I go where I can get the best deal. Also, I was invited."

For a minute there was silence. Maxim waited. The machine gun waited. The target waited, mutely dancing under the flares.

Then the short, bearded man spoke. "Continue the demonstration."

Maxim bowed his head in recognition. "Sir."

He motioned to his acolytes, who moved silently to either side of the machine gun, to ensure free running of the ammunition belt. He swept his pale gaze over the waiting group of Her Majesty's representatives, then turned his attention to the shining weapon. Experimentally he swung the gun smoothly from side to side on its swivel base. He peered through the sights, pointing the weapon towards the figures four hundred yards away which still danced silently in the uneven torchlight. I saw Maxim straighten his shoulders. There was a decisive click as he cocked the spring of the automatic firing mechanism, and he bent again to the sights, as his great finger sought the trigger.

A moment passed. The finger tightened. Like a clap of thunder when lightning strikes, the air was rent with sound. The slim barrel swung in a small arc, and in the twinkling of an eye the human figures dancing in the white light were annihilated. In the glare and the smoke, the nimbus around Maxim's head shone like a hellish beacon.

Within five seconds, the noise was over. The gun jammed.

# Chapter III
# The Man with the Shattered Arm

The ship's whistle sounded, thrilling every cell in my body, echoing from the broad walls of Liverpool's shipping warehouses, and sending the gulls screaming out far over the Mersey. From the white plume of steam at the ship's funnel, hot drops of water rained down on the immaculate afterdeck, startling anyone unwise or unfortunate enough to be standing underneath. Bright flags flew from truck and jack-staff, snapping in the fresh breeze from the estuary.

I had joined the *Etruria* the day before, and had been assigned my shipboard accommodations — a small cabin of my own, and a somewhat larger sick bay. I had checked over the medical supplies and the equipment with which the sick bay was stocked and, having met and spoken with my medical orderly, was satisfied that things were in good shape. Now, attired in my new uniform, I leaned on the rail of the upper deck and watched the passengers come on board.

In my youth, as I mentioned previously, before joining the Army I had served some months on a Pacific & Orient passenger liner, the *Orontes*, plying between Bombay and London. In those days it had been my pleasant practice to keep an eye out for unattached ladies, especially attractive ones who, travelling alone, might appreciate some extra care and attention from a dashing young assistant ship's doctor, during the extended voyage home through the Persian Gulf, the Red Sea and the Mediterranean. Today, no such lonely beauty appeared. Instead, the first-class gangplank appeared to be filled up largely with males, tweed-clad and red-faced. Two of them elbowed their way on board carrying newly purchased suitcases pasted with labels. They talked with flat Lancashire accents.

"So I told 'im fair and square. 'The price of cotton being what it is in America, if you want to mek a bit o' brass —.' Thank you, lad, I can look after my own bag." On their heels, a stout English nanny clutched a steamer blanket, a rolled umbrella and a large carpetbag. She shepherded before her a trio of fair-haired youngsters.

The boat-train from London also delivered our French-speaking and European passengers: fashionably dressed Quebec matrons, I should judge, returning home after a shopping spree in

Paris or London; exuberant family groups, chattering away nineteen to the dozen; soberly clad men of affairs, whose baggage carried hotel labels from half the cities of Europe. Cultivated Paris accents mingled with the rough-textured speech of the French-Canadians and with every accent of old England.

On the dock, crowds of would-be passengers tried to say their goodbyes and get to the ship. Friends and relatives, having come to see them off, tried just as hard to retain them for one last embrace. Hand trolleys bustled through the throng, trundling "Not Wanted on Voyage" cases into the 'tween-decks.

Into an open hold, cargo nets lowered wooden packing cases marked "Settlers' Effects."

As I watched this operation I saw a familiar figure standing rock-like in the flow of activity. Unmistakably, it was Hiram Maxim. I recognized the bear-like stance, the craggy features, the great black eyebrows, the shock of white hair springing out below the brim of a glistening top hat. He wore a black cape, and carried a rolled-up umbrella in the crook of his arm. At his elbow a port official, a flat cap on his head, was dwarfed by Maxim's stature.

Together they watched the cargo net swing its heavy load safely on board. Maxim signed a paper he held in his hand, gave a copy to the port official, and retained a copy for himself. Maxim seemed to be leaving England bag and baggage — and with the M-gun, by the look of it.

Scanning the crowd, my eye fell on another man who was also watching the loading operation. Dressed in worn Harris tweeds, he carried an all-weather ulster, a suitcase, a rucksack and a bundle of books. Maxim, lighting a cigar, turned and headed for the first-class gangway, and the man with the books followed.

I was called away from the upper deck to attend to my first patients: the chronic invalids, those requiring some special diet, those who needed reassurance against *mal de mer*. There was nothing serious, but it wasn't until we were well across the Irish Sea that I got my first breather. Darkness was coming on when I went on deck again; the engines had paused in their rhythmic thumping, and I saw that we were off the Irish coast, rolling gently in the trough of the sea. A lighter was manoeuvering alongside, rising and falling with the movement of the waves, its deck crowded with a huddle of men, women and children, carrying their worldly possessions, bundles of cloth, boxes and trunks tied with cord. The women wore shawls of wool covering head and shoulders; many cradled babies in their arms.

"Steerage passengers, Doctor." A quiet voice spoke at my elbow in an accent reminiscent of the Hebrides. I glanced at the speaker. It was the fellow with the books.

"The ship's whistle sounded . . ."

"Irish emigrants, bound for the promised land," I agreed.

An entrance port in the side of our ship had been opened, and light from the 'tween-decks fell across the hundred souls crowded on the deck of the lighter. As the sea surged between the two vessels, lines were thrown and secured, and, judging the moments when the deck of the lighter was on a level with the 'tween-decks opening, the emigrants jumped, scrambled, or were handed across. The gap between the two vessels constantly changed, rising and falling, opening and closing, spouting cascades of water, as if threatening those who sought refuge in our ship. I had seen this sort of thing before, in eastern waters, when a man misjudged his moment to jump, and got his leg mangled between the two vessels so that I had to operate on him. Watching the same manoeuvre being done carefully here, I hoped for the best, and it was accomplished without accident. The last to leave the lighter, flinging up bundles and bales ahead of him with his one good hand, was a powerful-looking, stocky, red-haired fellow. From the elbow down, his left arm was missing, and the stump was wrapped in bloody bandages.

Lines were cast off and the lighter sheered away. The steerage passengers safely on board, our ship's engines recommenced their rhythmic thumping. In a moment my orderly came up the ladder.

"The Irish lot are on board, sir. They seem to be in fair shape, bar some throwing up. But I think you should look at one of them. 'Bloody Red,' they call him. Him with the one arm."

"I'll come. Bring my case, would you?"

"Aye, aye, sir."

My orderly left. The bookish fellow who had spoken to me was still at my side. "'Bloody Red.' Now who would that be? A leader of some sort, by the look of him."

I turned on the fellow, ready to tell him to get about his business. He had removed his eyeglasses, and was using his pocket handkerchief to wipe off the sea mist. He looked up at me, and a faint amused smile crossed the tight Scottish mouth. Ginger side whiskers quivered slightly.

"The name is McIntosh. Charles McIntosh, after the Bonnie Prince."

Sherlock Holmes replaced his glasses and left.

I have said elsewhere that Holmes's career as a detective robbed the stage of a consummate actor. Impatient though I have been with him at times, he never fails to delight and fascinate me as he brings the theatre into my otherwise ordinary life. His presence on board at once changed the atmosphere for me. A man who a moment before had been just another Irish emigrant in need of medical attention was now brought to centre stage and put into the spotlight as "Bloody Red, a leader of some sort."

In the steerage section of the ship, the emigrants had already made themselves as comfortable as their cramped quarters permitted. Personal privacy being at a minimum, baggage formed semi-partitions behind which families camped. Clotheslines were strung, and shawls, blankets and clothing, wet from sea spray, were already drying. Babies were nursing, children settled in makeshift berths.

There was a cleared space in the middle of the deck, and above the thump of the ship's propeller I heard the cheerful sound of a concertina. A young son of Erin, his cap perched on the back of his head and his fingers flying, squeezed out a jig. Clogs and bare feet, at it they went, ten or a dozen of the poor Irish, dancing by the fitful light of the ship's lanterns.

I found "Bloody Red" seated on a pile of dunnage, a grim smile on his face. In his only hand he nursed an earthenware cup.

"I am the ship's doctor," I told him. "I've come to look at your arm."

He turned his sharp eyes on me. His accent was broad: "That's good of yez, sorr. Forgive my not gettin' up."

"No, no, you just stay where you are."

The medical orderly opened my kit. I sat on the deck beside my patient, and with surgical scissors cut away the rude bandages that bound the stump of his arm.

I had seen this sort of thing before often enough on the Afghan frontier — a man's arm shattered irretrievably. A miracle of creation, sinew, muscle and bone, the web of nerves, fingers which themselves could create miracles, play the concertina or violin, swing an axe, build a house, pen a sonnet or a love letter, press a maiden's hand in love, pull the trigger of a gun.

"Bit of a mess, sorr, eh?"

"What caused it?"

"Sharpnel, sorr. Rusty nails, from a homemade cannon."

I cleaned the wound and applied a dressing. He downed his poteen and grimaced.

"Ye've done this before then, sorr."

"Yes, I have."

"In the troubles, then?"

"In Afghanistan."

"I was thinking of troubles closer to home — Ireland."

"I'll give you something for this and see you again in a day or two."

"Thank you, sorr."

The dancers were still whirling as we left.

I had missed the formalities of dinner as I had expected, for the first night at sea was always a matter of sorting out and putting to rights. Suffice it to say that I did quite well with a bottle of hock and a few slices off the joint. After dining, I had barely retreated to my cabin and taken from my bookshelf a particular medical treatise that I wished to study, when there was a discreet tap on my door.

"Come."

"Charles McIntosh," said a soft voice. The door opened and the bookish fellow stood in the entrance.

"Do forgive me, Dr. Watson, but I was thinking what you were saying about the Scottish poets, and I thought perhaps — I have here — "

I was able to respond calmly after a moment of bewilderment: "Oh, yes. Do come in, Mr. — uh — McIntosh."

Holmes entered, closing the door carefully behind him. His voice, the very line of his body changed.

"Watson, dear fellow, how good it is to see you." He took my hand in both of his. "My word, it is like being, what does Dickens have Dornay say, 'recalled to life.' It is, really."

"Hello, Holmes. It is good, yes."

At times, when Holmes's usually reserved exterior drops from him, I am almost embarrassed by the warmth of affection that flows from him, and I find myself behaving coldly in response. Holmes felt that awkwardness as I put aside my medical treatise.

"It comes together, Watson," he said, putting his hands together like a tent, the long fingers intertwined. "It does come together." His eyes were shining.

"Does it, Holmes?" I had seen nothing to explain his euphoria.

"You had an opportunity, I take it, to sound out 'Bloody Red' O'Connell, the fighting Irishman." He sat on the edge of my bunk.

"Only in a professional capacity, Holmes. He needed a doctor's attention. I gave it to him."

"But you kept your eyes open, Watson. What did you see? A man of the soil, a peasant, a dull-witted bog-trotter? Or a man of letters, of sharp intelligence, learned in history? Aggressive, wary, open, friendly? What did his eyes tell you? His hands? Were they the hands of an artist or a workman, a scientist — "

"Holmes," I interrupted, "When I examined the man, he had but one hand. I paid no attention to the state of the calluses on it. My concern was totally directed at repairing his shattered arm."

"I'm sorry, Watson," said Holmes. "I am sometimes thoughtless in these matters. Do forgive me."

"If I may say so, you sometimes shock me with the ruthless pursuit of your goal. Individual human beings become mere pawns in your chess game."

He pounced upon me: "Watson, we are all pawns in games we cannot begin to understand. It is not my chess game. I am merely in it, and I must play it as well as I am able."

I shifted uncomfortably. A minute passed before he resumed.

"Now, the man 'Bloody Red.' Tell me about his wound. You did pay sharp attention to that, I presume?"

I chose to overlook his sarcasm. "The left arm was shattered below the elbow, probably a week or so before I saw it. It had been patched up efficiently, though crudely, as if in a battlefield operation. The wound was healing reasonably well. The man is healthy and strong."

"What caused the wound?"

"He said it was 'sharpnel,' from a homemade cannon firing rusty nails."

"Shrapnel."

"I supposed that was what he meant, yes."

"Was he firing it, or being fired upon?"

"The latter, I think."

"Why?"

"Had his own weapon exploded, he would have also suffered wounds in his face. I've seen it happen on the Afghan frontier, with crude copies of the Lee-Enfield the natives were using."

Out of a capacious pocket Holmes had fished a pipe and a tobacco pouch. "Would you say," he inquired, "that a wound like that could be caused by the victim experimenting with a weapon, a sophisticated weapon, he was unfamiliar with?"

I hesitated. "What kind of weapon are you thinking of, Holmes?"

"The M-gun, for instance."

He lit his pipe while I considered his words. "The ramifications of that question are a bit mind-boggling, Holmes."

"So is the context."

"The context?"

"Six thousand Irish Fenians assembling in the streets of Philadelphia, with fifteen thousand guns and three million rounds of ammunition. Others gathering at points on the American-Canadian border for the purpose of making an armed invasion, as they have attempted to do before."

"Good Lord!"

"The intention, just as in 1865, was to take over Canada and hold the country to ransom until Britain recognized their demands. They expected disgruntled Canadians to rise to their banner and throw off the British yoke."

"They didn't, of course."

"The leader was a fellow called John O'Neill, and his lieutenant a man known as Henri le Caron."

"A Frenchman?"

"No. British."

"The scoundrel!"

"He was a British agent."

"Ah! Spiked their guns, did he?"

"Yes, as a point of fact. He funnelled all the information back to British and Canadian authorities, and put a stop to the whole affair." Holmes drew on his pipe and shot me an amused sidelong glance. "We do have our uses at times, Watson, however unheralded."

"I don't see where Maxim fits in," I said after a moment.

"He doesn't fit in, and it's our job to see he doesn't."

"Well, what happened to the O'Neill fellow?"

"He disappeared back into the shadowy underworld that marks the Fenian operation. He was replaced by others — Jeremiah Donavan, Stephen O'Mahoney, the man they call 'Rossa.'"

"Is that Bloody Red?"

"Perhaps."

"He seemed a decent enough chap to me."

"Decent enough chaps, Watson, who conduct assassinations in Ottawa and in London. Who make repeated attempts on the life of Her Majesty. Who finance the building of torpedo-firing submarines intended to sink British shipping. In Skibbereen they call themselves the Phoenix Literary Society, in Paris the Committee of Public Safety, in Chicago the Fenian Brotherhood. It is a world-wide network, secret and subversive, dedicated to the overthrow of Britain. As you can see, I have been reading my notes from the Foreign Office."

"And you fear the M-gun will fall into their hands."

"I fear for Maxim himself."

We were interrupted by a knock on the door, and Holmes promptly resumed his role. "'Wee, sleekit, cowrin, tim'rous beastie,'" he intoned, "'O what a panic's in thy breastie.'"

"Come," I cried.

My orderly entered, "Excuse me sir, if I'm interrupting." He glanced nervously at Holmes.

"What is it, Jenkins?"

"Lady Edomé Boughton-Witherly requests your services, sir."

"Does she."

"Yes, sir." The man looked from me to Holmes and back again. *Mal de mer*, she says."

"You've tried the usual? Bismuth, solution of opium, arrowroot and wine — "

"Oh, yes, sir. Soup and cayenne, mustard pickles."

"And?"

"She wants your personal attention, sir."

"Then I had better go." I turned to Holmes. "Lady Edomé is one of the principal shareholders of Cunard."

"Then indeed you had better go, Doctor. Very wise of you, I should say."

I turned back to the orderly, "What is it that Sir Samuel Cunard says about seasickness, Jenkins?"

"'The only cure is to separate the passenger from the ship.'"

"Exactly. I shall come immediately."

The man disappeared, and I confronted Holmes.

"Look here. We have in this ship, in our less than commodious steerage compartment, one hundred and twenty-three souls — Irish emigrants, penniless, homeless, vomiting their guts out with every roll of the ship. You are asking me to fit these poor people into an evil plot of international magnitude."

Holmes fixed me with his grey eyes in the way he has when he wants to impress an idea forcefully upon me, and his voice was harsh. "Irish emigrants, Watson, most of them, want nothing more than a piece of land to call their own. But others want revenge for seven hundred years of what they consider English domination and cruelty, pestilence and famine. And a few of them will use any weapon to achieve their ends, including the M-gun if they can get it."

He looked at me a moment longer, closed his volume of Burns's poetry, and left me to my thoughts.

After a moment I found to my surprise that I was humming gently to myself. Edomé, after all these years! I hadn't seen her since those days and nights on the old *Orontes*. I got up and looked at my reflection in the mirror, wondering what she looked like these days. I took my old silver-backed military hair-brushes and applied them vigorously to my scalp, straightened my jacket and tie, and, with a light step, left my cabin.

# Chapter IV
# Suite A-13

In the evening the Grand Saloon came alive with conversation and music, the ladies adorned in the height of Paris fashion, the men elegant in evening dress. The English businessmen, with their talk of Manchester cotton and "brass," drank and played cards, while the French moved about in animated discourse.

Groups of men formed around the card tables to play *vingt-et-un* and baccarat. The ship did nothing to encourage gambling, but as the Prince of Wales once said, "Gambling becomes a vice only when done for stakes people cannot afford," and most of the passengers who flung down their counters on the turn of a card could evidently well afford it.

It was all very well for His Royal Highness to turn a *bon mot* on the subject of gambling, but the *Times* itself had expressed hope that the Prince would sign a pledge against playing cards. And the good Queen, in an attempt to stem public opinion against her son's extravagances, persuaded him to write a letter to the Archbishop, in which he was again neatly ambiguous: "I have a horror of gambling, and should always do my utmost to discourage others who have an inclination for it."

It does not take many transatlantic voyages, or trips to the Mediterranean or the Far East, in today's passenger steamers, to spot the professional gamblers. On this voyage I could identify at least half a dozen of them, some with titles, others getting by entirely on their wit and charm, like sharks cruising in a pool of unsuspecting minnows. My job as ship's doctor was ideal for Holmes's purposes, as it enabled me to move freely from one social stratum to another, without fear of detection, and to observe the gamblers as well as any other unconventional inhabitants of our shipboard world.

Maxim had quickly struck up an acquaintance with a dozen or more male passengers, who were attracted as much by his exuberant wit and tall tales as by his equally flamboyant performance at the card tables, where his forte was the game of *vingt-et-un*.

"Back home in the States," he said, "we call this game black-jack. Different name, same game. Sudden death in any language." And his massive head would come up in a malevolent grin.

Between rounds of cards, Maxim would hold forth to everyone in the smoking room, recounting his youthful forays from his small

"... I have a horror of gambling ..."

town in the State of Maine, U.S.A., across the border into the neighbouring Canadian province of Quebec.

He was fascinated by the French Old-World culture, the challenge of the turbulent northern rivers, and the beautiful young women of Quebec. It was the latter that got him into bloody fights, in which he seemingly gave a good account of himself, and eventually won respect and friendship among the tough French river men.

"Back home" in Maine, as a youth, he was an apprentice in his uncle's machine shop, where his remarkable native genius for invention had opportunity and freedom to grow. As we had already seen, that genius was now in full flower, one idea rushing upon another.

One of the gentlemen card players was a certain Baron von Kramm. His manner was as smooth and urbane as that of Maxim's was abrupt and blustering.

"I want to tell you, Baron," said Maxim at one point, not hesitating to expound his ideas, "your countryman Count von Zeppelin is barkin' up the wrong tree, with that dirigible design of his. It has no future."

"What then, sir, is the future, if man is to fly?"

"The future of human flight, Baron, is in heavier-than-air machines!" boomed Maxim.

"Heavier-than-air flying machines sound like a contradiction in terms, if I may say so. What would lift such a machine, and enable it to fly?"

"A system of what I call 'aero-planes,'" said Maxim, "concavo-convex, arranged in tiers, set at a slight upward angle to the horizon. So," he demonstrated with his hands, "with two large air screws propelled by a steam engine. The air screws push the machine forward at such a speed, that the wind pressure against the inclined planes overcomes gravity, and you fly, Baron, you fly!"

One of the English businessmen turned from shuffling cards to listen to the conversation. He appeared rather the worse for drink, thin, mousy strands of hair plastered against his forehead, his eyes unfocussed as he peered at the speakers.

"Have you developed such a machine, sir?" asked the Baron.

"I'm working on it, Baron, I'm working on it," replied Maxim.

"May I ask what is your fuel?"

"Naphtha gas, sir," said Maxim. "I've got seven thousand gas jets heating water in two thousand copper tubes, three eighths of an inch in diameter. Why, sir, in half a minute I can raise steam to drive a pair of two-cylinder compound engines, generating three hundred and sixty-three horsepower, and I'm here to tell you that is something that is really gonna put old England on the map!"

"England?" There was an edge of curiosity to the Baron's voice.

"Sure. Like your man Siemens, I find British patent laws very attractive."

"Too heavy, far too heavy!" interjected the bleary-eyed fellow.

"Sir?" said Maxim, turning to the speaker.

"Your flying steam engine."

"What?"

"I am Fred J. Wilkins, of the Manchester Iron Works. My firm manufactures steam engines, locomotives — "

"Good, sir. Excellent. You will understand, then — "

"But I keep them on terra firma, sir. On rails. On the ground." Mr. Fred J. Wilkins squinted at Maxim through the smoke from his cigar.

"That is the function of railroads, sir, is it not?"

"Are you telling me, lad, I should put wings on 'em, and mek 'em fly?" Wilkins guffawed loudly, looking around at the other card players for approval.

"I would be curious to know more of Herr Maxim's theories," said the Baron.

"I'm sure you would." Wilkins grinned maliciously. "Tek my advice, Maxim lad. Look out for the Germans. Any ideas you've got, keep them to yourself!"

The Baron's eyes flashed in anger and he half rose in his seat. Heads turned curiously. Maxim, to his credit, was quick to cover the embarrassment.

"No, no. The principles of flight are there for anyone to study. Four hundred years ago an Italian — "

"'Ere we go!" said Wilkins. "First the Germans, then the Yanks, now the Eyetalians."

"Sir!" Maxim turned his not inconsiderable bulk towards the offensive tradesman. But the blustering Wilkins had apparently wined and dined too well. A greater than usual surge in the motion of the ship was sufficient to set him off. He snatched up a table napkin, clapped it over his mouth, and pushing his way through the crowd made a beeline for a door leading to the upper deck.

The following evening a more pleasant diversion occurred. The *Etruria* was graced with an elegant curving staircase down which fashion-conscious first-class passengers could make a dramatic entrance into the Grand Saloon. In the adjacent music room was a Collard grand piano, which so far had only been used by the ship's small orchestra for after-dinner music. I was having a quiet brandy and a cigar before returning to my surgery to catch up on my medical records, when I became aware of a stir in the room and a murmur of French-speaking voices. Someone started to clap politely. I looked up to see the cause of the stir.

I have mentioned that in my earlier, romantic sea-going days I considered myself something of a connoisseur of female beauty, and had spent much of my free time cultivating the shipboard acquaintance of attractive ladies. I now watched spellbound, my brandy quite forgotten, as down the staircase came a young woman, so poised, so lovely in her movements, that I felt an actual physical pang of regret for times long lost. Her small, beautifully proportioned dark head was held high, showing an elegant line of neck and chin. Slender bare shoulders descended to a striking décolletage in the Paris fashion. Upswept dark hair disclosed small pink ears, from which diamond pendants sparkled in the light from the chandeliers, and around her throat a necklace of emeralds caught the light as she moved, and blazed with green fire.

The rhythm of her body as she descended the staircase brought a lump to my middle-aged throat. She must have caught my worshipping gaze, for as she passed she looked at me, and her mouth curved in a friendly smile. She went directly to the piano, and stood there for a moment until the clapping ceased.

The lady lifted her lovely head and looked around at the admiring company. Then she spoke, quietly but with confidence. "I was hoping I could pass unnoticed, but that was not to be. I have been asked to play for you. I shall do so now. Please forgive me if I am — how do you say it in English? — a little rusty." With a graceful sweep of her skirts she sat at the Collard and began to play — something by Lalo, I think, although unlike Holmes I am no expert on music — and I was swept up in the cascade of sweet sound.

It was not until the music ended, and the audience responded with a storm of applause, that the spell she had cast over me was broken. Only then did I see Maxim standing shadowed against the rich mahogany panelling, immaculate in evening dress, a sparkle of diamonds on his shirt front. He lifted a tulip glass to his mouth, and with the movement his leonine mane of white hair caught the light. From under heavy black brows, his pale eyes were on the woman at the piano. Then his head turned to look at the Baron, who like the rest of the audience appeared to be entranced by the music. There was malevolence in that look, and abruptly Maxim turned and left the room.

Holmes of course was seated close to the performer, the better to hear the subtleties of the music. He too had noticed Maxim's conduct, and gave an almost imperceptible nod of approval as I rose and followed the man's bulky form.

I know that in some quarters Beethoven's "Moonlight Sonata" is considered excessively romantic and self-indulgent. I do not agree, finding it, if a trifle sentimental, still thoroughly to my taste. And as I left the Grand Saloon I heard with nostalgia the yearning arpeggios with which it begins. The door closed behind me. On deck I found a starlit night, with a new moon glimpsed through the ship's rigging, looking to my eye sharp and curved, like a scimitar, a deadly Pathan knife-blade. The night air was cold, not surprising in these North Atlantic latitudes in April. We were moving at our top cruising speed over a calm sea, our wash painting a broad track astern of the ship. Under the sound of wind and wave and the ever-present throb of engines, I could faintly hear the fortissimo passages of the "Moonlight." But the deck was empty. I had lost my quarry.

A sharp click came to my ear, and I drew back into shadow. The door of a nearby stateroom opened, and into the corridor stepped Hiram Maxim, closing the door quietly behind him and passing close to me as he sought the upper deck. I noted the door he had left, "A-13," and followed him again into the night air.

Again I might have lost him, but in the lee of one of the ship's lifeboats I saw the flame of a match as a cigar was lit. In the darkness, I drew closer. Maxim was talking in low tones to someone I could not at the moment see. Over the wind I heard his coarse laughter and the occasional phrase in French, the rough eighteenth-century *patois* of French Canada. I caught the words '*au Saguenay*' and '*le roi*,' and Maxim used a vulgar phrase which seemed to amuse his companion.

Something changed hands. The other man moved briefly into the light, and was gone. He wore the blue jacket and watch cap of one of the ship's company.


In his tiny office, the junior purser was working after hours. He opened his door to me, shirt-sleeved, tie loosened.

"Hullo, Doctor. What brings you here? I thought you'd be in the posh section, eyeing the ladies. Whisky and soda?"

His South London accent was warm and reassuring.

"Are you offering me one?"

"What, on duty?" he joked. "Come in."

I entered the frowsty office. His things looked neat enough, but the ventilation was terrible, and I told him so.

"What do you expect with an inside cabin?" he asked, pouring me a drink. "The fresh air of Hampstead? Cheers."

Gratefully I accepted a glass of his excellent whisky, then sat down and wiped my mustache with the back of my forefinger, being careful of the curl. "Is your passenger list up to date?" I asked.

"I'm just finishing up. What with special rates for impoverished English gentry, and the fancy requirements of the French, I tell you, my work is cut out. 'Ees ze bathroom *en suite*?' 'Oh yes, Madame.' 'Ees eet equipped wiz ze latest — how do you say eet?' 'Ah yes, Madame, the very latest.' 'Also, my 'usband ees concern' for ze jewelry. Zere ees much — ah — stealing on ze ocean linaire.' 'Oh Madame, on the Cunard Line, we *nevaire* have thieves! But also of course, we have the ship's safe, for the valuables, *plus fort*!'"

"George, you should be on the stage," I laughed at his patter, enjoying my drink. "Tell me, who is in Suite A-13?"

George looked at me brightly.

"Aha! That's how the land lies!"

"Come along, man. Out with it!"

"I'm not sure you can get anywhere there, my boy."

"What are you talking about?"

"Madeleine de Vernisse."

"Who is that?"

"Where have you been? She is the toast of Paris, Vienna, Budapest — an internationally acclaimed beauty and concert pianist. She is on her way home from a tour that took Europe by storm. Crowned heads of Europe, and all that."

"Home?"

"Quebec City." George checked his file. "It was a late booking. We didn't expect her."

I peered over his shoulder, "I see Hiram Maxim's name there."

"The American. Yes, he is in A-15, next to la Vernisse. A big fellow."

"So I noticed. As a matter of curiosity, when was his booking made?"

George looked up the entry. "Back in February. There was some urgency about him getting to Quebec on the first sailing."

"Urgency?" I queried.

"I dunno," George grinned at me, "what d'you think, Doc? An affaire with Madame de Vernisse, the toast of Europe, sounds pretty urgent to me."

I could have kicked him. He saw the expression on my face.

"Sorry, Doctor."

"Thanks for the drink, George."

I returned to my cabin, not happy with my discoveries.

# Chapter V
# A Depression over Iceland

A depression over Iceland was given as the cause of the gale-force winds and heavy seas which now beset our vessel. Anything moveable was lashed down, and few passengers appeared in the dining room for meals. I was called to attend to the odd bruised elbow or cracked rib where someone had missed his footing or handhold in the unstable ship. About seasickness, the most common malady of all, one could do little but sympathize.

I attended Bloody Red O'Connell and attempted to lighten the lot of the other steerage passengers, so pitifully far removed from the graces and relative comfort of those with whom I spent most of my time. Bloody Red, like the rest, appeared to be grateful for what attention and relief I could give.

I learned a little more about him and the other emigrants. Some of them were taking up land in Ontario, south of the Georgian Bay, where Irish settlers, along with Scottish, had already cleared the land and put up log shanties in places given such nostalgic names as Tara and Duntroon. I was shown more than one pitiful little green sprig, growing out of a lump of Irish earth: a yellow briar rose, which they would plant again in the promised land.

Some single men were heading for the logging in the Ottawa Valley, closer to the port for which we were bound. "And what could be more of a man's life than riding the great log rafts down the Chaudière Rapids, and the like?" The pay was good, the rum was cheap, and on the weekends, by all accounts, there were some good fights to be had with the "French boyos." Bloody Red held up his stump of an arm.

"Fat chance for me now, eh, Doctor?"

"Not at all, O'Connell. You've got shoulders like an ox."

"I have that."

"And a good right arm."

"That, too."

"It is possible, you know, to build a sort of harness, of steel and leather, to fit over the stump of an arm like yours."

"And what good would that be, sorr?"

"It would give you a new hand."

"Holly Saint Christopher! Would it now?"

"An artificial hand, mark you. Or a steel hook. You will swing an axe with the best of them."

Bloody Red stroked his bandaged stump with his good hand. His eyes were on a distant point.

"A steel hook!" he spoke quietly, "I would bloody like that. By God, I would like that!"

I learned little more amongst the steerage passengers. Some seemingly hoped to get to America and join compatriots in such cities as Philadelphia and Chicago. But any hint of the Brotherhood, or the other secret societies that haunted Sherlock Holmes, was nowhere to be found. I began to wonder whether his imagination, so powerful in reconstructing the activities of a criminal, might in this case have conjured up a danger that did not exist beyond his own picturings.

I reported my observations to Holmes when I was able, adding, of course, the details of my pursuit of Hiram Maxim, the night of that impromptu concert by Madame de Vernisse. Holmes was always extremely attentive, checking me on obscure points, making notes, questioning me to see if I was consistent in my observations.

"Philadelphia, hm. Philadelphia. Very interesting. Most suggestive . . . Vermont? Maine?"

"No."

"No. That would likely be the French connection — and Maxim, of course."

Holmes would jot down another note, then turn his attention to refuelling that infernal pipe of his, leaving me as baffled as ever.

I should have been accustomed to Holmes's methods. He regularly assumed, or affected to assume, that because I had access to the same facts as himself, I could arrive at the same conclusions. "It is straightforward enough, my dear Watson," he would say, and then explain to me how it was done, making it seem so simple that I felt foolish. But for the life of me, I could rarely duplicate such feats. There were times also when I believed he kept certain vital information to himself, the better to savour the pleasure of revealing all at the last moment.

But perhaps I do my friend an injustice. We both knew that the French in Canada lived in uneasy tension with the English, unaffected by the relations between their mother countries across the Atlantic. Furthermore, Maxim's apparent fluency with Quebec slang, and his seeming relationship to Madame de Vernisse, were "most suggestive," as Holmes would put it. I was unhappy at the implications. I knew that I was breaking one of Holmes's basic tenets in allowing myself to become emotionally involved, but I could not help myself.

"The night of the big storm . . ."

The night of the big storm was the first time that I visited my friend in his cabin. Our previous meetings had been in my quarters, or in quiet corners on deck.

"Pretty posh, Holmes," I exclaimed.

"Is it?" he said, his head wreathed in tobacco smoke. He was deep in a book.

"Well, I happen to know it costs quite a bit." My voice sounded rather petulant.

"I suppose Her Majesty is paying for it," said he, turning a page.

"How do you explain it, considering your present role?"

"Role?" He did not bother to look up.

"The role of the impoverished professor of Scottish literature."

"Who said I'm impoverished?" He put his finger in the book to mark the place, and turned to me patiently. "Should anyone ask, which so far no one has, I am in fact travelling with a generous stipend from the British government, which is eager to cement relations with her colonies beyond the seas. I shall also get a modest fee from McGill College in Montreal, where I shall stay for a time as resident lecturer in Scottish poetry, literature and Hebridean folksongs. The latter is what I am now trying to study. I do wish I had my fiddle."

"I'm sorry I interrupted you, Holmes."

"Not at all, old fellow. I can be thoroughly rude myself." He put his book down, got his pipe going again, and looked up at me. "I might then lecture in America, and see what develops there." He picked up another volume from his book-littered bunk and leafed through it. "I am also getting frightfully interested in the legends and history of the Indian tribes, the Algonkian, the Ottawas and the Saguenay, and the rivalries between the English and the French for the possession of a continent. Also, since my unexpected return to life, Wilson Hargreaves of the New York Police Department will be inviting me — "

I did not respond. He broke off and looked at my miserable countenance.

"Sorry, Watson. I do go on. I sometimes wonder how you can put up with me."

I coughed and waved his smoke away.

"There. Thoughtless to a degree. And I am feeling the strain of doing nothing, waiting for days without knowing what it is that I wait for. I need a crime to investigate, a puzzle to solve — I was never made to watch without acting."

He put aside his pipe. "Do sit down, old friend. You look, if I might say so, a bit seedy. Brandy, perhaps?"

I waved away his offer, and sat down. Holmes produced a silver pocket flask, and unscrewed the cap.

"I am concerned about Madeleine!" I blurted out.

"Madeleine?" Holmes poured himself a shot of brandy.

"Madame de Vernisse," I said.

"Oh, yes, the woman." He tossed back the brandy.

"Damn it, Holmes," I cried, "she's more than 'the woman.' She is the most fascinating creature I've ever laid eyes upon. Delicate, sensitive — a creature not of this world of common mortals!"

"I say, Watson!" Holmes regarded me with dismay. "You are smitten!" The vessel hit a particularly heavy sea, which jarred her clear through. Holmes replaced the cap on his brandy flask.

"Yes, Holmes, I am smitten, as you put it. I've not had it so bad since I was a young man."

He regarded me with singular sympathy.

"Dear chap, I don't know how to say this, but Madame de Vernisse may be the key which unlocks this whole affair."

The ship shuddered again.

"Another pawn," said I.

"Can you not see it, Watson?" said Holmes losing patience, "Sometimes you really are a fool."

"I see a beautiful woman travelling by herself," I replied with some heat. "I see a fellow passenger — a brute of a man, Hiram Maxim — glaring at the lady in a cold venomous rage. I see this same man emerging from the lady's cabin in her absence, and in the darkness of night hand over something, valuable, I have no doubt, to one of the ship's company. Why should I not be concerned?"

"And now you want to blunder in, like a misguided Galahad."

"I only said I was concerned. I am not blessed with your cold detachment, Holmes!"

Sherlock Holmes looked at me, and took a long patient breath. The ship lurched again, and the newly patented Siemens Machine electric lighting system flickered.

"You have, I presume, observed the presence on board of Baron von Kramm, one of Europe's most notorious rakes."

"The presence of that suave fellow only serves to deepen my concern," I said miserably.

"Watson, for a moment, let us consider the evidence. In London, after the firework display, Maxim threatens to 'take the whole shebang' back to America, to use his uncouth phrase. Instead, he sails for Quebec, which is by no means in America. In Paris, Madame de Vernisse, according to your friend in the purser's office, makes a 'last minute booking,' and winds up in the cabin adjoining that of Maxim."

"So?"

"My dear Watson," cried Holmes, "sometimes you can be infuriatingly stubborn!"

"What about the Baron?" I said.

"You have noticed the emerald necklace that graces your lady's lovely throat?"

"I have."

"I happen to know something of the history of that necklace, and of the person who now wears it."

I did not respond.

"Do you want to know?"

"Not particularly."

Holmes looked at me and curbed his frustration. "I'll put it this way, Watson. If the Baron were one of the lady's European conquests, and he — "

"Preposterous, Holmes!"

"Such a liaison and such a gift could certainly explain the murderous look on Maxim's face that offends you so much."

"That is an outrageous suggestion!"

"How would you interpret the evidence, then, my dear chap?"

I did not know where Holmes's tortuous path was leading, but I had an inescapable feeling that Madame de Vernisse was being used, and that whatever unfortunate relationship she might have had with Maxim or the Baron von Kramm was not of her own choosing.

As I left Holmes and went out into the dark of the wind-swept upper deck, the ship again slammed into the trough of a sea, and for the first time in my life I was abominably seasick.


There is no better place to exchange intimate confidences than far from land, on the wind-swept deck of an ocean liner. Poised between two worlds, one left behind, the other yet to come, leaning on the ship's rail and gazing at the ever-changing face of the sea, two strangers, newly met, may reveal secrets to each other never before spoken of, even in the bosom of their families.

Thus I mused as, fine weather returning, I stood on the boat deck and watched the first-class passengers promenade below me. The object of my thoughts of course was Madame de Vernisse, the beautiful and talented young woman who had captured my fancy, all the more so now that Sherlock Holmes had placed her so firmly in the intrigue which surrounded us.

The ship was encountering smooth seas and fair winds this calm, sunny April morning, and from my viewpoint the spacious promenade deck was like a scene from the Champs Élysées. Elegantly dressed individuals, couples, bon vivants, families, strolled and stopped to chat, sipped cups of bouillon and sherry served by mess-jacketed stewards. Well behaved children bowled hoops and skipped under the watchful eyes of their starched nannies. On another deck, people tried their skill at quoits and shuffleboard. For those many who wanted simply to relax, reclining deck chairs were provided, each with a warm steamer rug. Occupying one of the latter, snugly wrapped in his blanket, was my friend Sherlock Holmes, reading a book. On the deck beside him were three more volumes.

Madame de Vernisse, the object of my fascination, was one of those engaged in a game of shuffleboard. With her were two young asses who, to my eye, would have looked more at home in the Tuileries Gardens than on the deck of an ocean-going ship. No matter. In an excessive display, one of the dainty young fellows fired off his wooden disc with such force that it effectively knocked the lady's disc clear out of the ring. It in turn slithered down the deck, and stopped only when it encountered Holmes's little pile of books. As he looked up, she turned towards him and spread her beautiful hands, her head on one side, and smiled an apology. Holmes started to untangle himself from his steamer rug, but she had swiftly moved to his side.

"Pardon, monsieur. Do not trouble yourself, please." She made a gesture towards the young gallants, who, pausing in their game, stood bowing and grinning like fools. "That young man, I think, likes to pretend great vigour — yes?"

Holmes got to his feet, book in hand, and gallantly addressed Madame de Vernisse in French: "Madame, I am only grateful to the young man that his excessive performance should allow me the pleasure of making your acquaintance."

She smiled. "Ah, what flattery, m'sieur. You speak French well. Perhaps with a Scottish accent, yes?"

"Thank you, madame. Yes. Scottish." He stooped and retrieved the wooden disc. "Allow me, madame."

"Merci, m'sieur. But what is this?" she picked up the book he had been reading. "*Légendes aux sauvages canadiens.*"

"Yes, madame. Do you know it?"

"Ah, yes m'sieur. My grandfather — you see the name. Are you studying it?"

"Part of my studies, yes."

"He wrote the book, my grandfather. He was in the woods with the *coureurs du bois* in early times."

"You are then Canadian, madame."

"Yes m'sieur. Of Quebec. Since the time of — before the English." She gave him a friendly smile.

"Or even the Scottish, perhaps." He gave her a little bow. Holmes can be quite the charmer when he wants, I thought.

She smiled, "Or even the Scottish. You will be studying in Quebec, m'sieur?"

"I hope to do so. For a short time."

"Then perhaps we will meet again."

"I do hope so, madame."

"*A bientôt*, m'sieur."

She turned, and with a graceful swirl of her skirt, left him standing there.

"Bouillon, sir?"

"What?" A steward had appeared at Holmes's elbow. "Oh, yes. Thank you steward. And sherry, I think." Holmes seemed quite pleased.

# Chapter VI
## Sherlock Holmes Makes Inquiries

In the character of the Scottish scholar, Holmes had been able to do nothing but observe our fellow passengers from afar. I knew that the inactivity chafed him, for his ill-tempered questions and remarks in my direction grew in intensity along with his desire to take a direct hand in affairs. At last he felt able to do so, at least to the extent of taking the captain of the *Etruria* somewhat into his confidence. Captain Walker smiled broadly through his white beard and welcomed us into his private quarters.

This will indeed be a story to tell my grandchildren," he was saying. "Sherlock Holmes on board my ship! How do you do, sir?" The fine fellow took Holmes's slender fingers in both of his own broad-palmed seaman's hands. "This is a great pleasure, sir."

He turned to me. "And you, you sly dog — our Dr. Watson, to be *the* Dr. Watson!" He laughed, boyish delight shining in his weather-beaten countenance. "May I offer you sherry, gentlemen? A nice Amontillado."

Holmes and I accepted with pleasure, and the old sea captain crossed to a locker which he opened with a small key.

"I have followed Dr. Watson's accounts of your adventures with avidity, sir, if I may say so."

"You honour us both, sir," replied Holmes.

I looked around the snug cabin, the organized space, with its gleaming mahogany and brass, its book-laden shelves. "A place for everything, and everything in its place." The captain saw my glance at a pile of well-thumbed *Strand* magazines.

"You are up there on my shelves, Doctor, along with Dickens and Stevenson. Dickens crossed on the old *Britannia*, you know. Didn't enjoy it. He returned in a sailing vessel. Can't say as I blame him." He found a bottle and some glasses. "That fellow, what's his name, the twenty-thousand-league fellow — ?"

"Jules Verne."

"That's him. He crossed on the *Great Eastern*. Wrote a book. Spent the entire trip on deck in a rocking chair." He poured the sherry. "Cheers. Gentlemen, please sit down." We did so.

"You, sir, Mr. Holmes — I was under the impression that you had departed this vale of tears. It was in the paper."

Holmes glanced at me. "That, Captain, is precisely what was intended. The impression."

"Oh, then — " the good captain looked puzzled and glanced from Holmes to myself and back again.

"Exactly."

"Ah." The old sea-dog sipped his sherry.

A few moments passed, punctuated by a muted chime from a polished brass-bound chronometer affixed to the bulkhead. "Hmm. Well then." He put down his glass on the table, and drew towards him a folder, which he opened.

Holmes tented his fingers in his familiar manner, and leaned back in his chair, his eyes on the captain.

"Tell us about gambling on the high seas, sir, if you will."

"Gambling. Well then, that's a subject! At its best, and that's the usual picture I might say, you meet these charming people, well-educated, courteous, entertaining. Sometimes an attractive man travelling alone, sometimes a couple — Lord and Lady this and that. You have a lovely trip. The only thing is you have bad luck at cards, or perhaps a piece of jewelry goes missing. Expensive, but perhaps you will know better next time. Perhaps."

"At its worst?"

"Ah! That's another matter, although we don't like to speak of it. Fortunes won and lost. Reputations ruined. Matters hushed up. Suicide."

"Suicide?"

"The cry 'Man Overboard' sometimes starts at the gaming table. If a man — or a woman — loses everything, including honour, suicide is sometimes considered the only way out, is it not?"

"What about murder?"

The old man's head came up and he looked sharply at Holmes. "Murder? Not in the gambling fraternity. Not in these waters. On a South American run, perhaps, a killing in a jealous rage, a family vendetta. It would be difficult to get away with a murder on board ship. Why would you suggest such a thing?"

"Never mind." Holmes turned the sherry glass in his long fingers, his grey eyes distant. "I have a feeling." His nostrils were pinched in the curious way he sometimes has when deep in thought. "I'll tell you this, Captain. I am personally charged with the safe-conduct of one of your passengers. I am responsible for his present safety and well-being, and his ultimate safe return to England."

"Ah. And he is a gambler?"

"He is indeed a gambler, sir. For the highest stakes. Far beyond the gaming table, or a quiet game of *vingt-et-un.*"

There was a pause, a silence filled by the ticking of the chronometer close at hand, and the surge of the sea outside.

"You fear for this man's life?" asked the captain.

"He is a man physically very well able to look after himself.

But like many a genius, he has a certain *naiveté* which may make him vulnerable."

"Blackmail, Mr. Holmes?"

"This man would not be vulnerable to anything as petty as blackmail."

"What then?"

"Political persuasion, sentiment, affairs of the heart. The rush of ideas, one upon another. His own erratic genius."

"Hmm."

The old man turned his bright eyes upon us. The face above the white beard and moustache was brown, seamed by forty years of sun, sea spray, and the winds of the world's oceans.

"Mr. Holmes, may I ask you, what are these 'highest stakes' to which you refer?"

Holmes took a moment before replying. "Power, sir. The balance of world power."

"And the man that holds these stakes?"

"Hiram Maxim."

"He is that powerful?"

"He is. And he may not even know it."

A moment passed. I was aware of the infinite sea about us, the rush of water past the side of our ship.

"Tell me, Captain, what do you know of the Baron von Kramm?"

"I have seen him from time to time. A traveller, a ladies' man."

"A professional gambler?"

"That's part of his trade. He appears to have commercial interests, which he does not speak much about. South Africa, Brazil. Last year I was on a South American run and he took passage from Rio to Hamburg. He was in company with a most gorgeous woman, I remember." He grinned widely.

"The rascal," I muttered.

"Oh, I don't know, Doctor. He seemed quite civilized to me. Knowledgeable of the sea and its ways. He'd been up the Amazon in some sort of boat."

"An adventurer, would you say?"

"An adventurer, yes."

"Was there not a story of theft of an emerald necklace from some Latin American country? Peru, Colombia?"

"There are always these stories. The Spanish steal from the Inca. A gentleman of fortune steals from the Spanish. A tottering government is held to ransom. The proceeds are used to finance a revolution. The revolution benefits powers-that-be thousands of miles away." Captain Walker drained his sherry glass. "Those emeralds are supposed to have graced the neck of every woman from Isabella of Spain to Madame de Pompadour, before coming to Madame de Vernisse. Poppycock!"

"Material for your next romance, Watson," said Holmes with the glint of a smile.

"I am keeping notes, Holmes," I replied.

The old man laughed and refilled our glasses.

"Why would the Baron take passage to Quebec, Captain?" asked Holmes. "That wouldn't seem to be his line of territory."

"Aha." Judkins leafed through the contents of his folder. His blunt forefinger stabbed halfway down a page of entries. "Here we are. 'Von Kramm, the Baron, *poste restante* Paris, Berlin. Embarked Le Havre for Quebec, final destination New York.'" He looked up at Holmes.

"That's a long way round to New York, wouldn't you say?"

Captain Walker smiled gently, his mild blue eyes without judgment in his seamed and bearded face. "*Cherchez la femme*," he said, "*cherchez la femme*, Mr. Holmes."

"Yes," responded Holmes, and he sipped his sherry. "One final question, Captain, if you will."

"Yes?"

"Fred J. Wilkins, Esquire. First-class passenger."

The captain again referred to his folder.

"Wilkins, Fred J. — Yes, here he is. Of Wilkins Locomotive, en route to Montreal. Business trip related to the Canadian Pacific Railway. Why?"

"Watson?"

"The man made a fool of himself," I said. "Insulting, boorish behaviour. Then, I might say, throwing up."

"What, in the Grand Saloon?" The captain was horrified.

"No, he contained himself until he got out on deck, I believe."

"Well then. Offensive, but hardly important."

"No," said Holmes, "but he did seem to overplay his role."

"His role?"

"Yes." Holmes shrugged. "Nothing more than that. Just a feeling. Probably nothing to it." He rose to his feet, and stretched to his full height. "Thank you, Captain, for talking to us. And, er — " He put a long finger to his lips.

"Mum's the word," said Captain Walker.

". . . a certain *naiveté* . . ."

Madame de Vernisse brought Chopin's *Valse Brillant in C* to a lyrical conclusion.

"That was divine, Madame, if I may say so. Quite magnificent," exclaimed Holmes.

"I agree," I said. "Most enjoyable."

"Thank you, messieurs." She looked at Sherlock Holmes from under her dark lashes. "I think you are also a musician, m'sieur?"

"Oh, I play very little."

"I think m'sieur is modest." Her tone was intimate.

"No, no, Madame. I assure you — "

"When I look at you, I see a *violoniste* of many years. One who has the passion for the *violon*, and will play for hours when he has the opportunity."

"Madame, you do indeed flatter me. How can you possibly know that?"

"From what I observe, m'sieur. Your left shoulder is held *un petit peu superior* — "

"Higher," I said helpfully.

"Higher than the right one. From many hours of practice." Holmes involuntarily settled his left shoulder. "There is a little lump under the left side of the — how is it — the *mâchoire*." She touched the elegant line of her jaw.

"Jawbone," I said, grinning at Holmes's growing discomfort.

"Yes, the jaw. From the pressure of the violin over a period of time. These things proclaim a practiced *violoniste*."

Holmes's face was a study. He had the look of one besieged in his own sanctum.

"Is there anything more you have observed, Madame?" He steepled his fingers and peered over them.

"The fingers of your left hand reach — how do you say — *plus loin de l'autre* — further than those of the right. Also, the tips of the fingers are more thick, *épaisse* a little, on the left hand."

Holmes looked at her a moment longer. Then the humour of the situation struck him, and he laughed uproariously. Madame de Vernisse smiled uncertainly.

"I trust I have not offended."

Holmes relaxed and took a deep breath. "No, Madame, no indeed. It is rare that one finds such perception. I congratulate you. You have penetrated my secret."

"M'sieur?'

"I do play the violin. I am a fiddler of jigs and country dances. A fiddler, aspiring to be a concert violinist — a follower of Sarasate."

"Ah, m'sieur." She smiled at him.

Our great circle course had taken us as far north as possible, consistent with safety, for we were mindful of icebergs. The wind was sharp and cold, and few passengers sought the upper deck, though visibility was excellent. I stood in the lee of a lifeboat, with an old pair of army field glasses.

The horizon on our starboard bow showed a glimmer of reflected light in the sky — the presence of ice, if I was not mistaken. Then, no more than a few hundred yards distant from the ship, a fully grown Greenland whale erupted from the ocean and crashed down again on its surface, sending spray sparkling into the sun. I moved to train the glasses on the gigantic creature. As I did so, I was aware, close to me, of a breath of French perfume and a light touch on my elbow.

I lowered the glasses and turned my head. It was Madame de Vernisse. In spite of myself, my foolish heart thumped like that of a schoolboy. Against the cold wind, she wore a long cape of mink or marten or some such fur, the collar of which turned up and made a hood for her shapely head. The hood was trimmed with fox, and from within its protection her eager face, full of wonder, looked out at the great whale. Her lips were parted, and I could see the vapour from her warm breath.

The leviathan spouted and plunged again.

"*Une baleine.*"

"Yes, madame."

"What a magnificent creature."

I looked at the lady's face, close to mine. On her dark eyelashes, moisture had settled in minute beaded drops.

"*Voilà!* There he is again!" She was like a child in her delight.

"Perhaps madame would care to look through the binoculars?"

She glanced at me, smiling. "I would like to, m'sieur, very much."

I helped to put the glasses to her eyes and focus them. The whale's tail came down on the surface of the sea with such a blow that I could hear the smack of it from the ship's deck.

"*Voilà! Merveilleux!*" She was breathing quickly. "How big is he?"

"Perhaps eighty feet. The biggest mammal alive." We were close together in the cold wind. "A unique creature in God's universe."

"How so, m'sieur?" She still gazed fascinated at the great whale.

"A thing of wonder, madame. In a creature so immense, the bones, the muscles, the nerves and the sinews of a whale's flipper are identical with the shoulder, and the arms, hands and fingers of the human being. Deep inside, one finds vestiges of what in some distant time must have been legs, for locomotion on land."

She lowered the glasses and looked at me with wonder in her eyes. "M'sieur, is that possible?"

"They are said to communicate with each other, hundreds of miles through the water."

"Swimming?" she smiled, joking.

"No, no. By some kind of perception. Sounds beyond the range of the human ear. Perhaps some kind of sympathetic vibration."

"Perhaps as in music." I saw that the diamond-like drops of water had gone from her lashes, no doubt wiped off by contact with the eyepiece.

"When one of them is in trouble," I said, my eyes on hers, "he sends out a signal, and others come to help."

"Is that true?" Her tone was neutral, suddenly guarded.

"They are hunted, madame. Those unique creatures. We human beings hunt them, for our own greedy purposes, almost to extinction." I longed to take her in my arms.

She looked at me intently for some moments before replying. "I must tell you, m'sieur. In this world, the hunting is not entirely confined to whales." Her voice was quiet but firm. "So one must be very careful. Thank you for your kindness."

She gave me back the binoculars, and I watched her descend to the promenade deck. My intention had been to offer her my help, not to receive obscure warnings about my own safety.

What was it that Holmes had said? "You blunder in like a misguided Galahad."

Was I such a fool? The binoculars retained a faint trace of her perfume. The whale had gone.

# Chapter VII
# Death in the Grand Saloon

"Where the devil have you been?" Sherlock Holmes can be ruthless in bringing one down to earth.

"What do you mean, where the devil have I been? I was taking a turn on the boat deck."

"You should be keeping an eye on Maxim, not on his mistress."

"Really, Holmes, how — ?"

"You are reeking of her perfume, and you are wearing a fatuous smile."

How Holmes could detect that faint delicate fragrance over the fumes from his pipe, I cannot imagine. Nor do I understand how he could reproach me for spending time with the same lady who had occupied his own attention the previous evening.

I composed my face. "Have I missed something?"

"An all but open quarrel between Maxim and the Baron."

"About what?"

"That is precisely what I wish to know," said Holmes. "There is a palpable tension between them that could erupt into violence. I fear for the consequences."

"Gambling losses?"

"Possibly."

"Rivalry over — the woman, Holmes?"

Holmes looked at me coldly through his tobacco smoke. Years ago he had been outwitted by a woman — an actress of great beauty, who at one point had been a consort of one of the crowned heads of Europe. She went by the name of Irene Adler. Holmes admired and resented Irene Adler, but he has never forgotten her. Perhaps the similarity to Madame de Vernisse was too close. Holmes chose not to answer my question.

"I would take it as a favour if you were to join them at the card table, Watson, and keep an eye open. You're an old hand at the game."

I suspect that Holmes felt a bit at a loss cut off from his usual sources of information: his Baker Street Irregulars, his confidential contacts in the criminal world as well as among the gentry, his efficient use of the telegraph and the newspapers, and his voluminous private encyclopedia. Indeed, I had wondered on occasion how he had survived without these familiar tools when abroad on those mysterious missions to Rome or Scandinavia to which he sometimes referred, but from which I had until now been excluded.

Holmes's reference to my being an "old hand" at the game, was true enough. As a young man, I had sailed back from Australia to England in an old square-rigger — one of the greatest adventures of my life. I handled sails and did my trick at the wheel with the best of them. We played what we called blackjack, clear across the Roaring Forties and around Cape Horn. Twenty-one-or-bust, *vingt-et-un* — it was the same game. Some fellows gambled away their pay for the past two years, then the very clothes off their backs, arriving in England penniless and virtually naked.

When I entered the smoking room, the game was in full swing. Ten or a dozen men were grouped around a baize table, betting on the turn of a card. The odious fellow from Manchester — Wilkins — had the bank. Players were "sticking" or "twisting" or "buying" or throwing in their hands with expressions of disgust. The atmosphere was tense. Tomorrow would see the end of the voyage. Today was a chance to make up one's losses, or to increase one's gains. There were glasses and bottles and the aroma of liquor, and the air was thick with smoke and the tension of the game.

As it happened, both Maxim and the Baron had lost their play, and thrown in their chips. I saw the Baron open his leather cigar case.

"Overplayed your hand again, eh, Baron?" remarked Wilkins as he raked in the chips. He talked loudly to be heard in the noisy room.

"There is always a next time." The Baron offered Wilkins a cigar.

"Thanks. You're a good loser."

"I usually balance the odds."

The Baron moved to join Maxim, and Wilkins put the cigar in his mouth. I noticed that despite the noise, smoke and drink, his eyes were clear and alert as they followed the passage of the Baron to Maxim, who was already in conversation with a slender Mediterranean-looking fellow.

"My grandfather was Admiral Caracciolo, Prince of Naples," said the latter in a raised voice.

"Yes?" Maxim's pale eyes were on the speaker.

"In 1799 he was hanged from the yardarm by your British Navy — " He sounded aggrieved.

"Not my Navy, sir!" said the American forcefully.

"The British Navy. Lord Nelson personally gave the order." The man's face was distorted with his cherished grievance over an insult to a noble family. "Ironically, we were allies against Napoleon."

"War is hell," said Maxim.

"Such an act should be repaid in blood."

"Every half-baked city-state in Europe has been paying off in blood for a thousand years. Where's it got you?"

"Warfare is a barbarous way of settling differences," said the Baron, "but when barbaric wrongs have been done, it is in human nature to avenge them in blood."

"The sacred blood of Germany," said Maxim.

"To me, sir, sacred, yes. Without that dedication life would be without meaning."

"You are too romantic, Baron." Maxim's voice was heavily jovial. "You are rooted in the manners of another time. And you too, if I may say so, Caracciolo. War today is simply another commercial investment. It is coldly calculated and paid for with the firm intention of getting back fat dividends and profits down the line."

"You lack nobility, *signore*," said Caracciolo stiffly.

"I see you as a man without loyalties, Maxim," said the Baron scornfully, "a crass arms dealer selling to the highest bidder."

The raised voices attracted attention. The game of *vingt-et-un* had broken up, and the players turned to this new diversion. I noticed Wilkins totting up his winnings; he struck a vesta, and held the flame to the cigar the Baron had given him, listening with interest to the altercation.

"See here, sir!" Maxim was flushed with anger. "You know and I know the realities. War today is big business, and the prize goes to the most powerful. The industrialized nations have to expand and control their overseas markets to stay alive. Britain and Germany are in the fiercest of commercial competition, and your Bismarck would not hesitate to attack Britain if he thought the investment was worth it. Nobility has nothing to do with it!"

"Take care, Monsieur Maxim!" The Baron's dark eyes glinted dangerously.

"That is why, sir," boomed Maxim, "Tirpitz has got the okay to shape up his grand plan for a supremely powerful German Navy. To challenge Britain's mastery of the seas."

The Baron maintained his composure. "If Germany builds a great navy to meet modern conditions, it will be to defend herself."

Over the Baron's words I heard a peculiar choking sound. I turned to see Wilkins, still at the gaming table, looking at me. Slowly his right hand went to his left breast. His mouth gaped open and from it fell his half-smoked cigar. His eyes bulged and fixed on mine. He turned up his last hand of cards: Queen, Jack, Ace.

"Twenty-one. The tides of spring," he said. Then he tumbled to the floor, scattering cards and drinks in all directions.

The Queen of Diamonds fell face up on the floor beside him. The Jack remained, crumpled, in his hand. The Ace fell on his chest.

By the time I got to his side, Fred J. Wilkins was dead.

I sent a steward hurrying to inform the captain, then raised my voice above the hubbub, hoping to allay undue speculation and concern: "Gentlemen, I am the ship's doctor." I paused to let them quiet down and pay attention. "As you may have noticed, we have had a bit of an accident here — "

This announcement was greeted with more than one hoot of unsympathetic laughter, and the odd comment: "He had one too many if you ask me," and "The fella's a bounder!"

"I must ask you to leave the smoking room at this time, gentlemen, so we may tidy the place up."

"Passed out, eh?" said Maxim at my elbow.

"Looks that way," I replied shortly, then lifting my voice again: "Come, gentlemen, please. You may take your drinks with you, I'm sure."

The men willingly enough left their places at the tables, the easy chairs and ottomans, and proceeded to clear the room, peering with curiosity as they passed the crumpled form of Wilkins lying under the table.

"Can I help, Doctor?" The offer came from the Baron von Kramm. He came quite close, and looked at the body and the surrounding debris with apparent concern.

"Thank you, sir," I said, "but naturally the crew is trained to handle this sort of thing." Maxim and Caracciolo had left the room in the wake of the others, but it was a moment or two before the Baron followed their example.

The main doors had barely been closed and locked behind them, when a personnel door at the far end of the room opened and through it came Captain Walker, followed closely by his first officer. Not entirely to my surprise, my friend Sherlock Holmes entered a moment later, followed by two orderlies bearing a stretcher and a sheet.

"If I could have a few minutes, sir," said Holmes to the captain. The Scottish academic had been replaced by the true Holmes I knew so well. He joined me beside the body, his grey eyes hawk-like now that the game was afoot.

"I saw the incident," he said. "What's your verdict, Watson?"

"I've not examined the body yet, Holmes."

"You determined the man is dead?"

"Yes, of course. At once. Before my eyes he fell to the floor. I felt for his pulse immediately. There was none."

"Have you smelled his breath?"

"He has none, Holmes."

"Don't quibble, man! His mouth!"

"I've done nothing other than feel for his pulse."

"Has anything been touched?"

It was the old Holmes again: sharp, intent, totally focussed on what was before him. He looked first at the disarray of the card table, the scattered counters of various denominations, the spilt drinks which still dribbled from the edge of the table onto the floor, wetting the forlorn body of Wilkins and the cards which his dead hand had dragged with him.

From one of the ashtrays on the table, Holmes delicately took a pinch of cigar ash. He rubbed finger and thumb together, feeling the texture of the powder. He did the same with ash from the second tray, then picked up a dead cigar butt, sniffed it, and returned it to the ashtray. Only then did he turn his attention to what lay under the table. He looked into the face of the dead man, smelled the open mouth, and scrutinized the hands, back and front, whipping out his magnifying glass to peer at the fingernails of the right hand. He took an envelope from his pocket, opened his penknife and scraped some invisible substance into it from under two of them.

Sherlock Holmes looked at the way the cards had fallen. Brandy from the table had dripped onto the Queen of Diamonds, so that she appeared to be weeping. On Wilkins's chest was the Ace of Hearts, and crumpled in his dead hand was the Jack of Spades.

"What did Maxim once say about the game?"

"He said, 'Back home we call it Black Jack, different name, same game. Sudden death.'"

"Suggestive, would you say?"

"Or purely coincidental, Holmes."

"Perhaps."

Under Holmes's lens, the face of the Queen leaped out in magnification, streaming with tears. From the dead man's grip, Holmes extricated the Jack — crumpled and torn half-across. He picked up the Ace of Hearts, and peered at it through the magnifying glass. He gave a grunt and passed it to me. In the centre of the Heart, sharply revealed through the lens, was a precise, tiny, but clearly visible pinprick.

As an old card player, one not totally unacquainted with the illicit practice of marking cards, I rubbed my finger across it. The minute bump on the back of the card caused by the pinprick was quite detectable to my finger tip.

"What do you make of that, Watson?" Holmes's grey eyes were upon me.

"It's a marked card, Holmes."

"Yes?"

"The rascal could certainly tell he had that particular card just by feeling it."

"Is that all?"

"What more is there? He had the winning hand. He won thousands of pounds over the voyage by similar means, I'd imagine."

"The Jack appears to be deliberately torn." Holmes was putting the playing cards into envelopes, which he labelled and stowed in an inside pocket.

"The man's paroxysm at the moment of death," I suggested.

"Would you lift his shoulders for a moment?"

"Right."

"Aha!" said Holmes. From beneath the body he retrieved the remains of the cigar that Wilkins had been smoking just before he had gone down like a sack of coal. Holmes picked up the cigar butt carefully, put his nose to it, and sniffed with dilated nostrils, for all the world like a bloodhound seeking a scent. He subjected it to intense scrutiny under his magnifying lens, eyes gleaming with satisfaction. Identification of cigars by their ash was a hobby of Holmes's which more than once in the past had brought a miscreant to justice. He had published a monograph on the subject, in which he specified the characteristics of some 140 varieties of tobacco, from Cuban cigarillos to Trincomalee cheroots and Burmese rat-tails. I had speculated from time to time that if, by any curious turn of events, men stopped smoking cigars, Holmes would be deprived of one of his most fruitful sources of deduction. Now he produced yet another envelope from his pocket, and tucked away the cigar butt for future attention. He spoke to the captain.

"I should like to go through the man's pockets in the presence of yourself, sir, and your first officer."

Captain Walker, the first officer and the chief purser had joined us. Wilkins's crumpled evening clothes revealed the labels of a Manchester gentlemen's outfitter. The tailoring was not top class, but acceptable. In a waistcoat pocket a gold hunter, attached to a rather ornate Albert, was looped across the well fleshed stomach. The fingers were ringless. In the man's inner breast pocket was a slim pocket book, containing little more than bank notes and a business letter from the Canadian Pacific Railway confirming a meeting in Montreal on the first of May. Holmes snapped open the back of the watch and scrutinized it through his lens, turning the watch this way and that. Finally he clicked it shut, his eyes hooded, and handed the timepiece to the purser, who added it meticulously to his list of personal items taken from the body.

I finished my medical examination, and straightened up.

"Well?" said Holmes.

"Heart failure," I declared.

"No foul play, then," said the captain with evident relief.

"I see no evidence of foul play, sir," I replied.

"Good," said the worthy captain, with a sidelong look at Holmes. "I am glad of that."

Holmes did not respond.

"Are you quite through here, Holmes?" queried the captain.

"Quite through, Captain. But I would appreciate a few words in your cabin, if I may."

"Very good. Number One, look after things, will you?"

"Aye, aye, sir," replied the first officer, and motioned for the stretcher bearers to come forward and remove the body.

# Chapter VIII
# The Solution of the Pine Box

"Please sit down, gentlemen." Captain Walker offered us a glass of his excellent Amontillado. "That's a load off my mind, I can tell you," he said, "not that I appreciate first-class passengers dropping dead in the Grand Saloon, mark you, for any reason, but when you were last in here, Holmes, you were full of dire forebodings of murder. At least we can rule that out." He lifted his glass in a salute. "Cheers!"

"I'm afraid not, Captain," said Sherlock Holmes.

"Oh, Lord!" The captain's sherry glass stopped halfway to his mouth, and he looked at Holmes, dismay written on his worthy countenance. "Lord," he repeated, gulping his sherry and pouring himself a refill before commenting further. "Mr. Holmes, Dr. Watson here, as ship's surgeon, has given me a verdict of 'death by heart failure' in this unfortunate matter. Are you challenging that verdict?"

"No, I am not," replied Holmes calmly. He settled into a leather easy chair.

"Then what are we talking about, may I ask?" The captain's manner was abrupt. Clearly, he was not pleased.

"As Dr. Watson has stated, the cause of death was indeed heart failure. But heart failure induced, I suggest, by chemical means."

Captain Walker passed a large square hand over his thinning white hair. He turned to me. "What's he talking about, Watson? Do you know what he's talking about?"

"Heart failure can be induced," said I, "but not in front of a roomful of witnesses. Not undetected. That is, not in my experience."

"So far, Watson," said Holmes with the glint of a smile.

Captain Walker sighed wearily. If Holmes had not been a detective, he might easily have been an actor or, if he had not wished to follow the Bard, a conjurer — a fellow who makes things appear and disappear under one's very nose. Part of the latter trick is something they call "dissimulation," I believe: distracting one's attention from the main issue by a bit of side play. Holmes was adept at it.

"Captain, you said that the Baron von Kramm had spent some time in the Amazon."

"What?"

"Baron von Kramm. Up the Amazon."

"Oh, yes, him. Some commercial venture, I believe. Where does he come in? I thought you were talking about a murder." He sighed again. "Oh, Lord!"

I knew that Walker had an unblemished record unique in the annals of sea captains, and wanted to keep it that way, for he was due to retire shortly.

Holmes took from his pocket one of the envelopes I had seen him secrete there earlier, and with a conjurer's flourish he produced the cigar butt he had retrieved from under the body of the unfortunate Wilkins.

"*Voilà!*" said Holmes.

Captain Walker looked with wide blue eyes at the battered half-smoked cigar that Holmes held up to view.

"A fine Brazilian leaf, beautifully cured, hand-rolled, one of the best cigars in the world, and of strictly limited availability. Indeed, even in Brazil it is a cigar smoked only by the privileged. The Baron von Kramm smokes them."

"Yes?" The captain's brows were furrowed.

"The Baron gave this particular cigar to Wilkins minutes before the latter's unfortunate demise." Holmes waved the tattered object at us. "Wilkins delayed lighting it until he had totted up his not inconsiderable winnings. Then within seconds of inhaling the first two or three lungfuls of smoke, he collapsed. His heart had ceased to beat."

The captain snorted impatiently. "Look here, Mr. Holmes, I'm told the fellow had been winning considerable amounts all the way across the Atlantic. He had also been drinking excessively. Such excitement in a choleric personality surely could result in heart failure without any additional cause, chemical or otherwise. Would you not agree, Surgeon?"

"I do agree," said I.

Holmes unlimbered his long frame. "Gentlemen, if I may."

He spread the envelope on the captain's table top, and placed the cigar butt upon it. From a waistcoat pocket he produced a sharp penknife, with which he carefully incised the cigar lengthwise.

"Look, Watson, what do you see? Captain?"

We peered at the dismembered butt. "Here, use my magnifying glass." I did so, and I discerned, running the length of the cigar and rolled into the fine tobacco leaves, a slender bright thread, pale as the underbelly of a snake, that seemed to shimmer under the Siemens patent electric light. Inured as I was to Holmes's bizarre disclosures, I felt a chill. This pale silken thread, he was persuaded, was somehow an instrument of sudden death.

The ship lurched in its passage, the light swayed overhead, and I was conscious again of the vast mysterious ocean surrounding us. I passed the lens to the captain. The old sea dog peered for a moment at the dismembered cigar.

"There's a thread of some sort in there. Not tobacco. Right?"

"Exactly!" said Sherlock Holmes. "That, gentlemen, is the agent that induced Wilkins's fatal heart attack!"

"In the upper Amazon of South America," said Holmes, "where the Baron von Kramm has recently been on his commercial ventures, are many strange, wonderful, and deadly things. Among them is a poison so powerful that a smear of it on an arrow, entering the blood stream, can cause instant death by paralysing the nervous system and so inducing a heart attack."

"I know about poison arrows, Holmes. In fact I've been shot at by the beggars." The captain scratched his beard and looked miserable. "Luckily, they missed."

"Quite. Then you will see my point, sir." Holmes turned to me. "Watson, if such a poison were ingested with tobacco smoke into the bloodstream, what would be the result, do you think?"

"Possibly a heart attack," I replied cautiously.

"Exactly. An induced heart attack. Undetected, undetectable."

"Gentlemen, gentlemen." The captain rose and paced the confines of his cabin. His voice, used to competing with the gales of the North Atlantic and Cape Horn, was controlled, resonating in the small room. "If what you conjecture is correct, Holmes, then I should have this rascal von Kramm put in irons and held for the shore authorities in Quebec. If it is not correct, and Wilkins simply collapsed in a fit of apoplexy stimulated by alcohol and the excitement of the game, and I arrest this Baron fellow, I could have an incident of international proportions on my hands, something I don't particularly care for, I'll tell you, after fifteen years of command!"

Holmes surveyed Captain Walker over the steeple of his long fingers. "Captain. Could you provide me with two or three live — rats?"

"Sir! Rats! Good Lord, man — on my ship?"

Holmes smiled at the captain's outburst. "Is it so uncommon, Captain, even in the best-run ship, to find the odd rodent or two in the bottom of the bilges?"

"What in God's name — ?"

"An experiment, Captain. A conclusive demonstration to put my theory to the test."

Captain Walker grunted and combed his white beard with blunt fingers.

"If they could be caught alive, and put in a box, say, a foot square," Holmes waved his hands sketching the proportions in the air, "and say six or eight inches deep. A box with a top to it to keep them from escaping. A sliding top, preferably."

"I suppose I could have Chippy knock something up," said the old man, suddenly chuckling to himself, "and I could rout a couple of those know-it-all apprentices of mine out of bed and get them chasing bilge rats, at —" he glanced at the chronometer gleaming on the bulkhead, "two o'clock in the morning."

The chronometer obligingly struck four bells.

"The sooner the better!" said Holmes.

As the grey light of a North Atlantic dawn showed through my porthole, a weary-looking, very junior ship's officer reported to my surgery bearing a sturdy pine box, from which came unpleasant sounds of claws scraping on wooden surfaces.

"Good," I said. "Just put it down on the operating table, will you?"

The young fellow did as he was told. He wore heavy leather gloves on his hands, and a sour expression on his face. His uniform showed recent signs of wear and tear. Elbows and knees were soaked with muck, forearms and back were streaked with red lead — a rust preventive commonly used to protect the lowest parts of a ship's hull. I thanked him, and dispatched him with my compliments to the captain to request his presence. Holmes rose eagerly from my settee and at once set to work.

"Now Watson, if I could have surgical scissors and a pair of tweezers," he said. "Thank you."

He spread out the cigar butt as before and laid the instruments beside it. From the closed box came muffled squeaks and scrabbling noises from the imprisoned rats. The captain stepped into the surgery, tying his dressing gown.

"Just in time, sir. I'm sorry to rouse you out of bed."

"Let's get on with it, then."

Holmes took the tweezers and the surgical scissors in hand. "From the cigar I am cutting about an inch and half of what I believe to be the lethal agent," he explained as he worked. "I shall extract it with the tweezers, and I would ask you to stand by, Watson, and to touch a match to it when I give you the signal. You must open the box a fraction so I may drop the stuff in, when lit. Then close the box again. Understood?"

"Right," said I.

The rats squeaked with renewed vigour, and the box jiggled on the smooth surface of the surgical table.

"Now!" said Holmes, holding up a pale strand in the gleaming tweezers. A vesta match flared. "I would advise you not to breathe for a moment." He touched the substance to the match. It caught and smoldered; a thin white sinuous smoke curled from it.

"Box!"

I slid back the lid a fraction. A rat's nose made brief unpleasant contact with my fingers before the smoldering stuff was dropped into the box, and the lid snapped shut. Holmes looked at his timepiece. The scrabbling and squeaks from the trapped rodents continued.

"One — two — three — and a quarter seconds," said Holmes.

The sounds from inside the pine box had ceased. We waited a minute or so in silence before cautiously sliding back the lid. In the box, three big grey bilge rats lay dead.

In the light of early morning we slid into the waters of the St. Lawrence. In muffler and topcoat I went on deck to find that the air had changed. It was softer, with a singular wild fragrance that buoyed up the spirits and made the pulse beat quicker. The rhythm of the sea had changed too, moving eagerly as if to set the ship more briskly forward on its course. In the confluence of ocean and river, we were entering on the flood tide.

The odour of pines now scented the air, as the great northern forests came to the water's edge. Here and there a strip of cultivated land stretched back from the river, with a few signs of human habitation. Passengers were beginning to appear on deck to get, for some of them, their first glimpse of their new land, and for others a welcome sight of home.

"At Father Point we take on the river pilot," Captain Walker had said. "I'll send off a message with the pilot boat for the Quebec authorities. In the meantime I'm afraid we have the unpleasant task of placing this man in custody."

I contemplated the problems of arresting a prominent first-class passenger — a titled man, furthermore — discreetly, efficiently, and without raising a disturbance or untoward concern amongst his fellow passengers. It was too late to catch him in the privacy of his stateroom before breakfast. He had already gone down to the first sitting in the dining room, and one could hardly clap the man on his shoulder between his kippers and his scrambled eggs, and haul him away in full view of his fellow diners.

In any case, there appeared to be little need for precipitate action, since the Baron was certainly ship-bound until we were alongside in Quebec. I suppose a case could have been made for alerting the Quebec authorities by way of the pilot boat and letting them arrest the fellow after we had docked, but the captain chose to do it otherwise. The first officer had two sturdy seamen to assist him in the arrest. They were provided with handcuffs, and the first officer himself carried a pistol inside his uniform jacket.

However, it proved not to be convenient to seize the Baron when, after a full and prolonged breakfast, he lit one of his Brazilian cigars and, blowing out clouds of fragrant smoke, casually joined the crowd forming on the deck to see the pilot boat come alongside. The pilot, a middle-aged Canadian, swarmed up the jumping ladder in a most agile fashion and joined the captain on the bridge. The Baron left the deck and made his way to his stateroom, where as he opened his door he was abruptly confronted by two burly seamen and the first officer.

The Baron hesitated not a moment, but with a cutting backhand sweep of his arm, struck the leading seaman a violent blow on the side of the neck, which tumbled that worthy into his fellow mariners. With his other hand, the scoundrel took a pistol from his inside pocket and backed slowly out of the stateroom. As chance would have it, Madame de Vernisse chose that moment to pass on her way to the upper deck.

"Bonjour, Madame," said the Baron.

"Bonjour, M'sieur le Baron," replied Madame de Vernisse, her eyes widening in shock as she saw the gun gleaming in his hand, pointing directly at her. He pulled her to him.

"You will accompany me on deck, if you please, Madame."

The first officer produced his own pistol and now had it levelled at the Baron.

"I shall not hesitate to pull the trigger, should you advance," said the Baron, who now had his arm around Madame de Vernisse in a manner which to the casual observer must have appeared unduly intimate. He moved her through the cabin flat and opened the door to the upper deck, his pistol concealed in the folds of her cape.

The foregoing sequence of events is my own conjecture, based on the statements of the first officer, as I was not an eye witness to them. Instead, I was on the upper deck amidst a throng of passengers at the moment the door to the cabin flat opened, and presented to my shocked gaze the Baron and Madame de Vernisse emerging for all the world like lovers in close embrace. Her distraught eye caught mine, and I pushed my way towards her. The Baron's eye was elsewhere, no doubt assessing the possibilities of escape, as I was pressed close to Madame de Vernisse by the surging throng.

"He has a gun!" she whispered, her breath warm on my cheek.

I hesitated. There was a gap in the crowd, and the Baron swept the lady towards the ship's rail.

As he moved, so did Holmes, of whose presence I had been unaware until that moment. With extraordinary swiftness and dexterity, his right hand moved speed between the two figures, so that the Baron's gun hand was swept up and Madeleine was thrust clear. She rushed into my arms as the gun fired, splintering a hole in a lifeboat overhead. With screams and shouts of dismay the crowd scattered. Holmes's left hand, used like a knife-edge in a gesture of the Japanese wrestling on which he prided himself, cut a stunning backwards blow under the man's nose. At the same instant the heel of Holmes's right foot swept the Baron's legs from under him. The man crashed to the deck, and would have been seized at once and put in irons by the first officer and his men, had not Maxim suddenly appeared. Holmes's baritsu tactics would have incapacitated a lesser man, but amidst the pandemonium the Baron retrieved his pistol and regained his feet, only to be attacked by Maxim, who rushed at him like a bull and grabbed him in a wrestling hold. The two big men, equally matched, struggled for supremacy, feet straining against the deck, neck muscles taut, faces contorted with effort and anger.

The ship's officer, armed though he was, could do little except await the outcome. On the bridge the Canadian river pilot sipped a mug of coffee, and the captain scratched his white beard with a patience born of his long years of experience. The pilot boat still lay alongside, awaiting orders. The ship continued to move upstream at a steady ten knots. The tide was on the turn.

Locked in each other's arms, the combatants staggered against the rails. The Baron still clung to his pistol as suddenly his knee came up into Maxim's groin. Maxim drew a swift painful breath and relaxed his hold. In a moment the Baron had broken away and was over the ship's rail in a superb dive. He curved in an arc towards the speeding frigid waters of the St. Lawrence, and as he splashed into the river, the vessel had already left him behind.

The captain stopped scratching his beard, and quietly spoke to the pilot, who lifted his speaking trumpet and called down to the pilot boat, a terse phrase in the local argot. In response, the boat turned away into the turbulence of the ship's wake, to attempt to pick up the Baron von Kramm.

# Chapter IX
# The Musician in the Tavern

It is not unusual for a death to occur on board ship during a transatlantic voyage — or a birth for that matter. Indeed, during the days of sail, now thankfully giving way rapidly to modern steamships, unfortunate emigrants were packed in their hundreds into airless insanitary spaces below decks. Ships were buffeted by contrary winds and weather for weeks on end. Food and water became scarce and contaminated, and epidemics of cholera or typhoid could break out, so that on arrival in Canada, those who had not been buried at sea would have to be confined in quarantine until they were given a clean bill of health, or until death overtook them.

Near the Victoria Tubular Bridge, built largely by Irish immigrant labour in the 1860's, and spanning the mighty St. Lawrence River at Montreal, that "Eighth Wonder of the World," is a great rock that had been dragged out of the turbulent stream. On its massive granite face, deeply inscribed, are these words: "To Preserve from Desecration, the Remains of Six Thousand Emigrants, Who Died of Ship-fever in 1847-1848."

Such tragic loss of life by "ship fever" no longer occurs, thanks to the application of modern medical knowledge, strict cleanliness and diet, and thanks also to the innovation of steam and of iron which in so few years have changed the nature of travel. A transatlantic passage that could take nine weeks or more in a sailing vessel is now a predictable eight or ten days in a steamship.

The whole nature of shipbuilding, perforce, has changed. The famous shipyards of Quebec, which for two hundred years had rung to the sounds of the broadaxe and the whipsaw, have become virtually silent. The songs of the carpenters and riggers are heard no more. The immense log booms of prime Canadian oak and pine, rafted down the St. Lawrence River to Quebec, are now squared into timbers for export to England. Ironically, it was here in a Quebec shipyard that a vessel was built that anticipated, perhaps hastened, the demise of the great days of sail. The *Royal William*, in 1833, became the first vessel to cross the ocean powered by steam alone.

As the *Etruria* manoeuvered in midstream, amidst the St. Lawrence traffic — the local steamers and ferries, smart river schooners and squat barges — a log raft came surging towards us on the outgoing stream, held barely in check by a steam tug. Like a great wooden carpet spread upon the surface of the river, those hundreds of logs, pegged and bound together with chains in an intricate and flexible cross-pattern, had come down from Ottawa, or perhaps Prescott or Kingston on the Great Lakes, running the infamous rapids of the Long Sault and the Coteau. There were about thirty men riding the logs, picturesque in spiked boots, red sashes and stocking caps. They manned an assortment of long sweeps or oars, which they worked in unison measured by a cadence of song, bending their backs to control their ungainly steed.

The raft was big enough to accommodate two shanties — a cook house and a bunk shelter — on its heaving surface. Half a dozen square sails were rigged on slender poles thrust between the logs. Bright flags and pennants flew above them, snapping in the freshening breeze. Such a raft would have been on the way for perhaps two weeks, changing crews at different points on the journey — some Irish, some French. At Lachine, Indian pilots would have been brought on board to help navigate those legendary and hazardous rapids.

Watching this colourful scene, I stood for a moment on the upper deck, overlooking the steerage deck below. The Irish emigrants were up in force, bag and baggage, ready to go ashore. I heard a shout, and turning my head I saw Bloody Red O'Connell waving up at me with the stump of his arm, his red hair like a flame. He gesticulated at the raft and its occupants.

"That is a man's life, sorr!" he cried.

"Indeed it is, O'Connell," I shouted, "and the best of luck to you!"

I had given him a letter to the port health authorities in Quebec, who I hoped would provide him with an artificial limb, thus giving him a chance in the future. I returned his wave.

"See Quebec and live forever. Eternity would be too short to weary me of this lovely scene." Thus writes William Kirby in the opening lines of his famous historical Canadian romance, marvelling at "this bright Canadian morning, worthy of Eden, this glorious landscape worthy of such a sun rising."

Would that I had leisure to linger on the scene he describes. We had no sooner got alongside the docks of Quebec, the monumental Citadel looming overhead on its magnificent pinnacle of rock, than customs and immigration officials swarmed on board to facilitate the movement of our shipload of passengers. Steam trains — great iron monsters compared to our tidy British equivalents — hissed and clanked onto the dock, hauling wooden coaches to carry our emigrants westwards to lumber camps and cities, to farms and

". . . the Victoria Tubular Bridge . . ."

wilderness and prairie, a thousand miles and more into the heart of this immense country.

I was busy with my staff checking out the routine health matters and documentation, discharging passengers under my care. I had seen two individuals — officers of the Quebec police, I judged them to be — go to the captain's quarters, where I suppose they were informed of the death of Fred Wilkins, late of Manchester, and of the "man overboard" incident of the Baron von Kramm of Paris and Berlin. I say "suppose" because I heard nothing more about the matter. My original assessment of Wilkins's death by heart failure was documented, and that was that.

It was not until late in the day that I regained the deck and saw the efficient manner in which our hundreds of passengers, bag and baggage, had been transferred from ship to shore. The loaded trains screeched and emitted clouds of steam as they began to move, the new arrivals leaning out the opened windows, the better to savour the event. The engines were equipped with great bells, like those of a church, which tolled lugubriously, adding to the din. The dock was a hive of activity as loaded carts moved off with baggage and cargo. Well appointed carriages, drawn by spirited horses, welcomed the return of the Quebec residents and packed them into comfortable seats with their hand baggage up behind. Families were reunited with laughter and tears. Of Maxim and Madame de Vernisse I saw nothing. Holmes, too, had vanished.

I had barely packed my own bags and paid my parting respects to Captain Walker when a gangling urchin in the characteristic Canadian hat called a tuque sought me out and gave me a grubby piece of paper. It was a note from Holmes: "Have gd accom at inn, Le P'tit Cochon Qui Rit. Follow Aristide."

I looked at the bright-eyed gamin: "Aristide?"

"*C'est moi, m'sieur.*"

"*Bon. Allons-y a Le Cochon Qui Rit,* Aristide," I said, summoning up my rusty French. Aristide cheerfully shouldered my old steamer trunk, and we left the ship.

Quebec City was more extensive than I had expected. Wharves and docks to accommodate a fleet of ships filled the shores below the cliffs. Shipbuilding yards, now sadly neglected, abutted the timber yards, and merchants' warehouses extended for miles along the waterfront. The old town, below the Heights on which most of the city was built, reminded me of St. Malo in France. It dated from the seventeenth century, with its stone houses, the curved eaves to the roofs. A jumble of streets and alleyways, an open market and a precipitous ascent known as the Breakneck Stairs led to the more formal Upper Town of grand houses, châteaux, churches and public buildings.

It was to a narrow street in Lower Town, secluded and not too far from the river, that Aristide led me. Amidst a collection of stone houses built against the face of the rock, Le P'tit Cochon proved to be a snug retreat from which issued such delightful smells of cooking that I realized I had had little to eat since an early breakfast. As we approached, I heard the sound of a fiddle which repeated the phrase of a melody two or three times, then went on to another phrase which it repeated. Then it backed up and repeated the lot. Aristide shifted his load and flung open the door.

I stepped inside and saw the source, or rather the sources, both of the Inn's name and of the music. Upon entering, I nearly tripped over a small pig, which scuttled towards me across the sawdusted flagstones of the floor. This induced laughter from three or four men who occupied the low-ceilinged parlour. Grouped together around a sturdy old refectory table, and illuminated only by the pale light from a side window, they could have been a study for an Old Master. Three dark-eyed Canadians looked up at me. Two of them wore the familiar tuque stocking-cap of the countrymen. One had a fiddle under his chin. The third had an apron, signalling his role as proprietor. The fourth member of the company also held a violin. His grey eyes caught mine for an instant and winked at me before he turned back to the matter in hand.

"*Encore*, m'sieur," said Sherlock Holmes.

The *habitant* with the fiddle at once obliged, and launched into the melody I had heard in the street. Holmes joined in and was shortly improvising around it. A middle-aged woman of generous proportions entered with tankards of freshly drawn cider, and was promptly seized around the waist by my young pilot, Aristide. Laughing and protesting, she delivered her precious cargo to the table before joining him in a jig which seemed to me as much Irish as French.


Darkness had fallen, and through the window in the two-foot-thick stone wall I could see the lights on the shipping in the harbour. I had a snug bedroom under the eaves of the inn. It contained a small spindle-bed covered with a colourful patchwork quilt, the work no doubt of my landlady. On the floor of wide boards lay a woven rag rug. A crucifix and a coloured picture of the Virgin Mary adorned the white-washed walls. In a corner stood a small rocking chair, with a seat fashioned like a tennis racquet. Against the wall was a small table, and there were hooks on the back of the door on which to hang one's garments. Aristide had brought up my steamer trunk.

There was a tap on the door. It opened and Holmes joined

me, puffing at his pipe and expelling clouds of acrid smoke.

"Good Lord, Holmes, what are you smoking?"

"*Habitant tabac*. These enterprising people grow it themselves." He closed the door.

"I think it is even more aromatic than your customary shag," I said, opening the casement.

"Yes, I think it is," he replied happily as the smoke made a wreath around his head. He took a paper and pencil from his pocket and sat on the bed, humming the while.

The night air came in at the window, bringing with it the fresh smell of the river and the scent of pine trees.

"Jolly good dinner, I must say," I offered conversationally. "Eel stew, *tortière*, cider. Jolly good calvados. They make it themselves, you know."

"Yes. I thought you enjoyed yourself." He was jotting notes on his sheet of paper. I waited a moment.

"Holmes — "

"Could you hold off a moment, old chap? I am just writing down a tune here, while it is fresh in my mind."

I grunted, and turned to the window again. The moon, in its first half, was breaking through ragged clouds. In the flowing river, lights were reflected from the moored ships. The tide appeared to be on the ebb, increasing the force of the current so that the ships tugged at their moorings. Holmes at last put away his paper and pencil and spoke up cheerfully.

"You see before you, Watson, a student of the music of *les canadiens, les gigues, les* songs of the *voyageurs* and of *les rafteurs*. I am finding a remarkable relationship between the music of *le canadien* and le Scot and le Irish. I shall likely write a monograph on the subject — " He broke off. His pipe had gone out, and he looked around for somewhere to deposit the dottle.

"Holmes — " I said again.

"Yes, old chap?" He had found an earthenware dish and used it for an ashtray.

"What are we doing here?" I demanded.

"Doing?"

"What about Maxim? What about Madame de Vernisse? What is the upshot of the Fred Wilkins affair and the escape or the recapture of the Baron von Kramm? What about the dark purposes of the Fenians? While you are happily fiddling away, I must admit to you that my mind is in a whirl. I trust yours is not."

He looked at me, his eyes twinkling. "Ah, what would I do without you to keep me up to the mark, my dear Watson?" He slumped back on the bed, and pulled the bolster up, the better to accommodate his head.

"It might be useful to us both, you know, if you were to bring me up to date," I said.

He beamed at me for a moment. "Right you are, Watson." He steepled his fingers, his eyes closed. "First, our charge Hiram Maxim. He and his lady — "

"His lady?"

"Madeleine de Vernisse."

I snorted, and Holmes opened an eye to survey me patiently. "Come now, Watson. They have been friends since childhood." I did not respond. Holmes closed his eye again and continued.

"As you know, Madame de Vernisse is aware of my interest in French-Canadian folklore, legends, songs and so on. She was good enough to recommend this modest but charming hostelry as suited to my needs while researching those subjects here in Quebec."

"That's nice."

"It's more than 'nice,' Watson." The eyes snapped opened and the voice sharpened. "You asked for information! Philomel, my fellow musician in the tavern, is not only an excellent fiddle-player, he is also a storehouse of information. He works in the one shipyard in Quebec that is at the moment functioning. He has access to the foundry and to the machine shop. He tells me that Maxim's packing cases were delivered there late this afternoon."

"The M-gun," I said.

"Not necessarily," replied Holmes. This surprising remark dispelled the last of the effects of the calvados.

"Not necessarily, Holmes! Then what have we been chasing? I thought Maxim had his infernal invention with him, 'the whole shebang' as he put it, and you were supposed to induce him to take it back to England where it belongs. That is our purpose, Holmes, is it not?"

"Our purpose is to keep an eye on Maxim and see that he doesn't get into trouble. To observe, to understand, and to act when the moment is opportune."

As a doctor I have been trained to be as precise as possible in my diagnosis of a condition, and to relieve the problem by direct action ranging from medical treatment to surgery. Holmes's patient, indeed cavalier, attitude, his exotic methods, his inclination to withhold analysis and intended action until he chooses to divulge it, all run against my nature, though I have lived with them for years. I took a deep breath.

"Before I left the ship, I expected to be questioned by the authorities with respect to the death of Wilkins, and the disappearance overboard of the Baron von Kramm. But no questions were asked."

"Wilkins's death appeared to be from natural causes, and

presumably the Baron was fished out of the river by the pilot boat. Perhaps Captain Walker considered it wisest not to have the matter probed further. I gather he has had a blameless career, and would hardly want to sully his record unnecessarily."

"Holmes, you and I know that whatever Wilkins's death appeared to be, it was not from natural causes. You went to great pains to prove that he was deliberately done in by the Baron. For what reason, that's what I want to know."

Holmes smiled at me and raised an eyebrow. "He was cheating at cards?"

"Really, Holmes, is that likely?"

"You implied it yourself. The marked card — "

"Half the players at that table were card sharks!"

"Oh?"

"A gentleman does not commit murder simply over a card game. This is not the American Wild West. A duel, perhaps — "

"Then what do you think, old friend?"

"I think the Baron had reason to silence Wilkins."

"Yes?"

"Which means that Wilkins was privy to information the Baron did not want disclosed."

"Bravo, Watson!"

"And that means that Wilkins was something other than what he appeared to be."

"Quite," said Holmes.

"Which leaves me with one observation, and one question," I continued.

"And they are?"

"If the official verdict on Wilkins is 'death from natural causes,' then the authorities have no reason to hold the Baron. And if he survived the frigid waters of the St. Lawrence he will be after you like a wounded tiger."

"That possibility has not escaped me," said Holmes drily. "I shall endeavour to be ready for him. What is your question?"

"If Maxim's packing cases do not contain the M-gun, what the devil do they contain?"

"That is what we shall find out."

"How?"

"Through Philomel. Or perhaps through Maxim himself. We are invited to dine at the Château de Vernisse tomorrow."

"... a calèche ..."

# Chapter X
# At the Sign of the Golden Dog

The sun was well down in the western sky as a *calèche* took us by a circuitous route to surmount the great cliff which separates Upper from Lower Town. Our able driver navigated a network of narrow streets and hairpin corners, passing busy taverns and restaurants, and threading his way through considerable traffic, until at length we turned into the quiet retreat of the fashionable Rue de Buade and drew up before a handsome eighteenth-century stone residence.

A warm glow of light shone from the windows, and the scent of wood smoke hung in the air. Holmes paid off the driver, who clucked to his horses and moved off down the street. I paused before the imposing edifice, feeling inadequate for the coming encounter. My dinner clothes needed the services of a valet, and I feared I would not cut a very handsome figure at Madame de Vernisse's dinner table. At least my collar was clean, I assured myself, and my cravat was decently tied. When I turned to see whether Holmes looked as seedy as I felt, he was standing with feet apart, peering with considerable curiosity at a square stone, set into the wall of the building.

"What do you make of that, Watson?" he asked quietly.

I moved beside him to see what had captured his interest. Carved into the stone was the figure of a dog, covered with gold leaf which glittered in the gathering dusk.

"Curious," I said.

"Quite," he replied. He whipped out his magnifying glass.

"It's a funny-looking bone he's chewing."

Holmes leaned closer to the carving. "It is intended to represent a human thigh, I believe," he said.

The door to the château had swung open, and a ray of light fell upon us from the interior.

"It *is* a human thigh, McIntosh."

We turned to the voice. Standing massive in the doorway, impeccable in evening dress, stood Hiram Maxim. "I guess those eighteenth-century Frenchmen had a great sense of humour," he said with a rumbling laugh.

"There are some lines of poetry here." Holmes's voice had resumed the soft Hebridean lilt. He read aloud, peering at the stone: "'*Je suis un chien qui ronge l'os, en le rongeant je prends mon repos. Un temps viendra qui n'est pas venu, que je mordrai qui m'aura mordu.'"* He looked up at Maxim, "What's all that about, do you suppose?"

"I am a dog that gnaws his bone," said Maxim. "I crouch and gnaw it all alone."

Holmes was peering again at the inscription. "A time will come, which is not yet — "

"When I'll bite him by whom I'm bit," Maxim concluded. "Crazy Frenchmen. Look at the date: a hundred and fifty years ago! Come on in, gentlemen." We moved towards the open door.

"You're not thinking of biting someone, are you, Maxim?" said Holmes in good humour, putting away his glass.

"Only if I'm bit," responded Maxim, "and nobody's tried that yet."

As we entered, an elderly retainer took our cloaks and hats. Into the reception hall, down an elegant curving staircase, swept our hostess. It was the Grand Saloon all over again. I had eyes only for Madame de Vernisse. The swirl of a black velvet gown set off her creamy skin and the line of her neck and shoulders. Precious stones glowed at her throat and ears, and in her dark hair was a diamond ornament which caught and fractured the light from the candelabra into a thousand pinpoints of incandescence. Her smile was warm upon us.

"Welcome, gentlemen. It is so good of you to come. Please, please come in. There is a nice warm fire. Although it is May, it is still cool in the evenings, is it not?" Her delightful voice flowed on, modulated, as soothing to me as warm honey. I realized how long it had been since I had been in the warmth and welcome well-being of another's home, let alone one so charming as this.

Hiram Maxim had preceded us into the salon. Tapestries hung on the wall, along with paintings of hunting scenes which I liked, views of *habitant* life, and family portraits of stiffly posed gentry, clothed in the fashion of a hundred years earlier.

One portrait in particular caught my eye, that of a young woman of great beauty, who bore a singular resemblance to our hostess. The artist had captured the same eager tilt of the shapely head, and the same elegant line of neck and shoulders. On the ornate frame was inscribed "Amalie de St. Luc, Baronne de Charlevoix." It was dated 1793.

"My grandmother," said Madeleine de Vernisse at my elbow. "She is lovely, is she not?"

"There is a remarkable resemblance, if I may say so, madame." I gave her a bow, and she smiled at my clumsy compliment as if I were a poet and a court gallant rolled into one.

I turned again to examine the painting. In the shadows, balancing the composition, but not at once drawing the eye, the artist had painted a small round pedestal table of some elegance. Upon it was a box of red velvet, which revealed the presence of an old-fashioned, silver-mounted duelling pistol. A shadowed indentation in the velvet marked where its matched companion would normally lie. The fingers of Amalie's left hand were poised on the edge of the table. Her right hand, partially concealed by the folds of her gown, held the missing weapon, pointed at the floor. On Amalie's face was a quiet smile.

"It was painted in the days when Edouard, Prince de la Grande Bretagne, lived here."

"Edward?"

"The Duke of Kent." It was Holmes who spoke — I was surprised, for he generally affected to know nothing about rank and society. I looked from Madeleine to the portrait and back again.

"For two years he was the Colonel of the Regiment of Royal Fusiliers stationed here in Quebec. He was the father of your Queen Victoria."

There was a tinkling sound of fine crystal, and the manservant came into the room bearing champagne glasses and a bottle. My hostess moved away, and the moment was broken. Once again I was left with more questions than answers.

"Allow me," said Maxim to the old fellow, seizing the bottle in his great hands. In a trice he had the wire binding off; the cork was released with a resounding pop, and the sparkling glasses were filled.

"Champagne," said Maxim.

"To you, M'sieur McIntosh, and your research," said our hostess. "Doctor, your good health. M'sieur Maxim, to you and your dreams. May we all be blessed."

We sipped the excellent champagne in the warmth of friendship. Presently Madame de Vernisse took Holmes lightly by the elbow.

"I have something that may particularly interest you, m'sieur," she said with a smile. She guided him to an alcove where a Broadwood grand piano stood. A candelabra shed a pale light on its gleaming surface. Piles of music occupied nearby shelves, and on a bookcase rested a violin case of black wood.

"*Voilà*, m'sieur, *une violon*. Tonight we will see if you are just the country fiddler you claim to be."

Holmes's grey eyes gleamed with pleasure. "May I, madame?" He reached for the instrument case, snapped open the catch, and lifted the lid. From its nest of worn velvet he lifted out an instrument which he caressed with gentle fingers.

"Beautiful," he breathed. "The proportions, the wood, the varnish! Above all, the workmanship, Italian, certainly. From the 1690's I should say. Quite possibly Antonio Stradivari of Cremona — Stradivarius himself!"

"Bravo!" Madame de Vernisse clapped her hands together in delight. "So much for the country fiddler! Until after dinner then, m'sieur."

Maxim was talking expansively, "First time I came up here to Que-bec, little more than a boy, I was on the loose from my uncle back in the States. He kept my nose to the grindstone, you might say, in his machine shop. I figured there was more to life, so I went a-roving. I was a pretty good artist and I made a few dollars decorating carriages for the gentry. Gold leaf and red lacquer, very pretty." He laughed and poured another glass of champagne. "That's how I met this lovely lady and her daddy. We would take a couple of canoes and explore the wild rivers around here. The wilder, the better. Remember, *cherie*?"

Madame de Vernisse nodded, her eyes bright. "I remember."

"I was always drawing things, I was always interested in how things worked. Carriages, flying machines — "

"M'sieur Maxim is an inventive genius, you understand," said the lady, gently mocking.

"A birch-bark canoe!" exclaimed Maxim. "Buoyant, strong, light, easily repaired! What could be more elegant? Flotillas of canoes — hundreds of them. Ten men to a canoe, each boat carrying two tons of freight right from here, up the St. Lawrence, fighting their way past the rapids. The Ottawa, the French, across the great Georgian Bay, three hundred miles of open water to the head of the Lakes. North to the rivers that flow into the Arctic Ocean! The fur trade that opened up half the continent!"

"You did that, Maxim?" I asked innocently.

"Not me, Doctor — are you kidding? That was years ago. Her people did, though." He gestured at our hostess in his rough manner.

"In the old days," said our lady, "the *seigneurs* of my family travelled in their canoes past the head of the Great Lakes, and discovered the headwaters of the Mississippi River. They followed it a thousand miles south to the Gulf of Mexico, and claimed all that land for the Kings of France."

There was a pause in the conversation, a silence broken only by the flutter of the flames from the fire.

"In this house there are storerooms of great size, which for over a hundred years were constantly packed to the rafters with riches from the wilderness. Beaver pelts of great price, silver fox, mink and bear skins, ermine to trim the robes of kings and princes, all waiting shipment to the fur markets of Europe. The Citadel of Quebec was the French fortress of America, and this house of the Chien d'Or was at the centre of it."

"And then the gol durn British took the whole shebang," said Maxim.

*"Ah, les anglais — un temps viendra"* — her eyes were dark.

There was another silence, in which the line of doggerel ran in my head: "A time will come, which is not yet, when I'll bite him by whom I'm bit."

The manservant silently entered and announced dinner. Maxim emptied his champagne glass, and we moved into the adjacent dining room, where a Louis XIV table, clothed in damask and glittering with silver and crystal, awaited us. Candlelight reflected the delicate yellow of spring daffodils in profusion, arranged in vases and in bowls.

"As a young fellow I worked in the New York Ironworks and Shipbuilding for a while," Maxim said. "I got interested in the triple-expansion turbo steam-engine and suggested a few improvements."

A clear soup was served, and Maxim continued to talk as he spooned it to his mouth: "I got Tom Edison real mad at me one time a few years back. I was working on the principles of the incandescent electric lamp and lit up the whole durn town of Filchburg, Massachusetts. Electricity was supposed to be Tom's bailiwick, but I got there first. By the time he caught up, I was onto something else." He laughed.

"Would it be proper to enquire what you are working on now?" asked Holmes. Maxim finished his soup.

"Wa-al, sir, I've been thinking some about underwater propulsion. Everybody else is doing it. Nordenfeldt in Sweden. Goubet in France. He built a dinky little thing that can stick a torpedo under a ship's keel and blow it up. He sold a bunch of them to Russia." Maxim inclined his leonine head to our hostess. "Excuse me ma'am, if I offend your sensibilities."

She smiled and gave me a charming shrug, "Doctor, why are you men so fascinated with blowing each other up?"

"Some are of the opinion it is in our God-given nature, madame," I said. "The instinct for survival."

"Instinct for murder," she said, her eyes clouding.

Maxim plunged on, "Down in the States, the War Department is putting up money for research into submersibles. The Smithsonian got two hundred thousand dollars to come up with something. Even those crazy Fenians financed the building of a submarine of sorts, and launched it on the Potomac within sight of the White House!" He laughed again, and dabbed at his mouth with a damask table napkin.

"Fenians, sir?" said Holmes.

"Disaffected wild Irish. There's thousands of them in the eastern American cities."

Maxim talked, and one delicious course followed another. A *paté* of goose liver that rivalled anything of Prunier or the Cafe Royal; trout amandine; spruce grouse, served with tips of asparagus and a grain that was introduced to me as wild rice; a serving of venison whose rich taste was nicely set off with tender "fiddleheads" — the first curling spring shoots of the wild fern. With each course appeared French wines of a delicacy for which Holmes, in the character of a Scottish scholar, could barely hide his admiration. Madame de Vernisse did her best to guide the conversation to music or the wonders of European travel, but Maxim had fixed ideas about human competition, conflict and war. Holmes, had he wished, could have diverted the conversation in the brilliant way he had, into any number of channels, including some of the most recent developments in science and in chemistry, touching closely on Maxim's work, had the latter but known it. But he was content to play the part of a good listener, nudging Maxim along from time to time, though the man needed little encouragement. Finally, as we finished the meal, our hostess broke into Maxim's monologue.

"Gentlemen, I shall leave you to coffee and liqueurs. Should you wish to smoke, there are cigars on the sideboard."

She rose and withdrew. Holmes and I sat down again, and Maxim reached for the cigars. The quiet manservant poured the coffee and left us to ourselves.

"Cigars, gentlemen," said Maxim. "Excellent Cuban leaf. Thanks to the Nova Scotia trade with the Caribbean."

Fresh in my mind was the "excellent Brazilian leaf" that had so neatly disposed of the late Fred Wilkins.

"I shall stick with my pipe, if I may," said Holmes, sipping his coffee.

"Doctor?"

"Thank you, but no," said I.

"You don't know what you're missing." Maxim selected a cigar for himself, and with sharp white teeth neatly bit off the tip. He lit up and continued his line of thought as we helped ourselves to brandy and liqueurs. "As I was saying before the lady left us, I deplore war. No man in his right mind could approve of war as a solution to human problems. And yet we constantly indulge in it."

The end of his cigar glowed and the white ash lengthened as he inhaled a lungful of fragrant smoke. He looked at the ash thoughtfully.

"I deplore war," he repeated, "but I believe there is a solution. I believe that the prospect of war should be made so appalling, so frightful, that no nation will ever declare war on another, because to do so would invite its own destruction." His words, spoken in quiet resonant tones, chilled my soul. In the drawing room our hostess was playing what sounded like a Chopin waltz. Holmes sat very still, listening to Maxim's disturbing proposition, his eyes hooded.

"Consider, gentlemen." Maxim was standing with his back to the cheerful fire. By his manner he might have been discussing plans for a picnic on the river. "Consider an airborne fleet, capable of hovering over London or Berlin beyond the range of mere ground-based cannon. Such mobile heavier-than-air machines might be equipped with devastating weapons, which could rain death down on precisely selected targets. Surely such a device, with its promise of mutual destruction, would impose a state of peace upon the world."

Holmes's voice was cold: "As an inventor, Maxim, would you not then be challenged to build a bigger and more powerful cannon to shoot the machines out of the sky?"

The big man gave Holmes a calculating glance. A laugh rumbled up from his chest, and he flicked the lengthening ash from his cigar into the fire.

"Check, McIntosh," he said. "So what is the solution to this everlasting contest?"

"We might try changing the social conditions that are the causes of war," said Holmes.

But Maxim had fished an envelope from his pocket, and with a stub of pencil was making arithmetical calculations on the back of it. I doubt that he even heard Holmes's quiet suggestion.

If my friend Sherlock Holmes had any misgivings about playing the violin for Madeleine de Vernisse, that beautiful and talented concert pianist just returned from her triumphant European concert tour, he did not display them.

In our years of acquaintance, I had grown used to Holmes's manner of extracting melancholy chords from the instrument, sometimes droning on for hours on end. Occasionally, to please me I think, his fingers would render some recognizable tunes such as Mendelssohn's *Lieder*, but his recitals, in my experience, had never been for an audience, particularly one so knowledgeable and critical as this one. So it was with some trepidation that I saw him tune the rare Stradivarius to concert pitch and run through a few finger exercises. Our hostess sat at the keyboard in quiet repose, waiting until he had warmed up. Were I a painter, I would have painted them then, illuminated by the fire and the candlelight in that gracious setting.

Presently Holmes leaned over and spoke quietly to Madeleine de Vernisse. She nodded, and in a moment her white hands moved over the keys in a cascade of rippling arpeggios. Then the violin entered, clear and exquisite, playing a sweet melody which I could not identify. I listened entranced and, somewhat to my surprise, with a growing sense of envy. For, at the moment, it appeared to me that my dear friend Holmes, and the lovely lady to whom I had lost my judgment, inhabited a private world of their own making, complete, perfect, excluding all else.

Hours later, we regained our lodging. Through my open window a waxing moon cast a pale light on the surface of the St. Lawrence. The tide was ebbing, and the eternal battle between the ocean and the stream had swung for the time being in favour of the latter.

My eye followed the moon's path upstream to the west, the route of those incredible French newcomers, the forefathers of Madeleine de Vernisse, who two hundred years ago had paddled their frail canoes into the wilderness and founded an empire three times the size of Europe. I thought of that beautiful lady, the toast of international capitals, who, returning to her ancestral home, seemed now to be haunted by the shadows of bygone times, an empire lost, and a patiently vengeful Golden Dog. I thought also of my old friend Sherlock Holmes, who in all the years of our acquaintance had avoided the company of the fair sex, claiming that women diverted his mind from the cold logical processes so essential to his nature and to his occupation.

As I watched the moonlit path on the river, a great log boom came into view, travelling fast with the combined speed of the river current and the outgoing tide. I lifted binoculars to my eyes, and there on the surging logs that leaped magnificently on the turbulent outgoing stream, I could see human figures, *les rafteurs*, under the billowing makeshift sails, bending their backs to the great sweeps. On the night air, above the rush of the great river, I could hear their voices raised in bold, nostalgic song: "*En roulant ma boule roulant, en roulant ma boule. . . .*"

I remembered Bloody Red O'Connell, deep in the steerage of the *Etruria*, with his smashed arm and his dream of a good life in the Canadian woods. And his words, "What could be more of a man's life than riding the logs down the Chaudière Rapids and the like?" What indeed, O'Connell! Was he still one of the pawns in Holmes's game?

# Chapter XI
# A Telegram from Home

When I went down to breakfast the following day, Holmes had already finished and had gone out into the spring morning. I was comfortable in a window seat, enjoying a second cup of coffee and taking advantage of Holmes's absence to bring my notes up to date, when he returned, stooping his tall frame under the low lintel of the doorway.

"I see you are writing up your notes, Watson. Sensational as usual, I presume." Holmes sounded disputatious. He was smoking his long cherry-wood pipe, rather than his blackened clay — a sure sign of a dark mood. He slumped into a chair at my table and called for coffee. Our landlady quickly obliged, and as quickly withdrew.

"Perhaps a little fuller account than usual, Holmes," I said.

"Full of your fanciful embellishments and attempts at colour and life," he grumbled.

I reined in my tongue. "Holmes," I said carefully. "You perhaps forget the number of times, at your request, I have reduced the 'embellishments' as you call them. I have had to disguise the real players and the dates and the very locations of your dramas — "

"Exactly!" he retorted. "You present them as dramas, rather than confining yourself to the cold observation of cause and effect."

I had heard this sort of thing from him before, and tried to be patient.

"This is a pretty sensational series of events, Holmes, you must admit — "

"I see little point in flaunting the sensational and the *cause célèbre*," he said. "I would rather you dwelt on the everyday incident, with particular attention to an examination of logical synthesis and the faculties of deduction that I have made my special province."

I must say that I am repelled by the egotism which seems to be such a strong factor in my friend's singular character.

"I really must protest, Holmes," I said. "You would have me write a course of lectures on 'the Holmes Method,' while you go off on your own to sort out affairs of state — *causes célèbres*, if you will, in Holland, Denmark, Odessa, the Vatican — and come back loaded with honours. I begin to suspect that your trip to Sweden was to keep an eye on a certain illustrious personage during the trials of the Nordenfeldt submarine. And was it pure coincidence that you happened to be in Constantinople some months later, when that vessel was delivered to the Turks?"

Holmes looked at me through his tobacco smoke with cold detachment.

"Meantime, I am left at home to write up your everyday incidents!" I went on, in full spate. "Well, I shall do you justice, as usual, but I'm going to use my own discretion in what I write, and how I write it. Call it sensation if you will."

"Bravo, Watson!" said Holmes, "I trust you can get it published." He finished his coffee in a single draught and flung himself out of the room.

No longer comfortable, I sat in my window seat for a few minutes after Holmes had left. I lit my own pipe, and brought to mind how on a similar disputatious occasion he had criticized my work by saying, "In avoiding the sensational, Watson, you may have bordered on the trivial." Really, there was no pleasing the man. I could only suppose that his cold detachment from things emotional had been somewhat disturbed by his intimate encounter with Madame de Vernisse the previous evening. I packed away my notes and set out for a brisk walk along the waterfront to blow the cobwebs from my mind.

"Watson, be good enough to look at these and tell me what you see," said my friend.

I was diverted from the medical treatise I was trying to read. Holmes was smoking his blackened clay; his mood had lifted, and once again he resembled the eager hound in close pursuit of his quarry. We were sitting in my room.

"They appear to be the cards you retrieved from Wilkins's body," I said.

"What else?"

"Twenty-one. A winning hand."

"Yes?"

"The Queen of Diamonds is stained with brandy. The Jack of Spades is mutilated and torn half-across. In the centre of the Ace of Hearts is an almost invisible pinprick."

"Tell me again, Watson: before Wilkins collapsed, what exactly happened?"

"He looked at me, his eyes bulging. The cigar fell from his mouth. He held up those three cards and said, 'Twenty-one. The tides of spring.' Then he fell to the floor, scattering cards, drinks and counters in the process."

"Not 'tides of fortune' or 'Ides of March.' How about 'the torrents of spring'?"

"No. The tides of spring."

"Why did he turn to you when he spoke? You were not in the game."

"No, I was only looking on."

"Then he was trying to tell you something."

"I doubt he was thinking very clearly at that moment."

"I believe he was thinking very sharply indeed," said Holmes. I closed my medical treatise and put it aside. "There was a letter in Wilkins's pocket from a Mr. I. Sinclair of the Canadian Pacific Railway, confirming a meeting that was to take place between them in Montreal. I have been in touch with Mr. Sinclair, and I have a coded telegram in return which identifies Wilkins, not as a manufacturer from Manchester, but as an agent for Her Majesty's Government."

"I see," I said, although many things were not at all plain to me. Holmes had his magnifying glass in hand; he subjected the cards to intense scrutiny.

I rose and went to the window. The view it afforded of the river never failed to please me. The paddle-wheel ferry, bound across the river for Levis, set a course angled upstream to counteract the current. The tide must be on the ebb, I thought. But my heart was heavy. I had read the riddle of the cards.

"So we must take it that he knew the functions of both me and you," said Holmes, "and he had information to impart to us. Information important enough — "

"To die for!" I concluded.

"Exactly, Watson. Look at the cards again and tell me what you see." He looked up at me.

"I don't need to," I said, staying where I was.

"Oh?"

"I think I know what they signify."

"Tell me."

"Assassination. A bullet through the heart."

"Assassination of whom?"

"Her Majesty. At the time of her Diamond Jubilee, I should think, before the crowned heads of Europe, the assembled maharajahs and sultans of Empire."

"No, Watson, I don't think so. Not yet, anyway."

"What, then?" I turned to him.

"An event much closer in time and place." Holmes's finger jabbed at the mutilated Jack of Spades. "An attempt on the life of the Prince of Wales, the heir to the throne." His voice was harsh.

"Why, for God's sake?"

"Revenge. Settlement of ancient feuds. Or one of a series of outrages calculated to wring out political concessions. Or the act of a madman. Take your choice, Watson. Such things happen. The Queen barely escaped death at the hands of a Fenian anarchist at least once. A Canadian Member of Parliament was killed by a Fenian pistol shot a generation ago."

The ferry to Levis had successfully made its crab-like crossing and was at the docks on the further shore. I watched the movement of the other craft in the freshening breeze: schooner-rigged coasters, canoes, a tug which had been nosing a log raft into the shore. The tide was slackening.

"Tides of spring," I said.

"What the devil does that mean?" Holmes shot at me in exasperation.

"There are 'spring tides,' Holmes."

"Well, what the devil are 'spring tides'?"

"The highest tides of the month, caused by the influence of the moon, in conjunction with the sun."

"When do they occur?" barked Holmes, suddenly like a terrier at a rat hole.

Years ago, Holmes had said that he did not care whether the sun went around the earth or the earth went around the sun. He said he didn't wish to clutter the attic of his brain-box with useless information. I smiled at the memory.

"What are you grinning at?" snarled Holmes.

I did not mean to tantalize him, but he had often had me hanging on his deductions from his observed facts which I had failed to see; I relished this moment when matters were reversed.

"Holmes," I said, "look out the window and tell me what you see."

He crossed and peered out. "The confounded St. Lawrence River."

"What else?"

"A lot of boats coming and going."

"What is the state of the tide?"

"Damn it, Watson! I have no idea what is the state of the tide!" He flung himself back across the room. "All I know is that the future King appears to be threatened, and I don't know when or where to look for the danger!"

Rarely had I seen Sherlock Holmes in such a state. He did not like it that I should be better informed on any subject than he was himself, no matter how little it might interest him.

"Holmes," I said after a moment.

"Yes, Watson?" he grunted.

"Is there any more information I do not know about?"

For answer he thrust his hand in his pocket and pulled out a crumpled cable, which he flung at me. I picked it up and smoothed it out. Under the dateline London it read thus: "BERTIE GONE AHUNTING HA HA COWS FIRST LIGHT TODAY REGARDS MYCROFT."

Holmes had, on occasion, referred to his brother Mycroft, who held a mysterious position of authority with the British government — who was, one might say, himself the British government.

"What the devil does Mycroft mean by that?" my friend demanded. "Even at the exorbitant rate of a shilling a word for cablegrams to Canada, he might have been more forthcoming."

# Chapter XII
# The Tides of Spring

On the crisp morning air came the sound of bells, announcing an early service for the Roman Catholic people of this chiefly French city. Housewives passed on their way to market, longshoremen on their way to the docks. Carts loaded with farm produce were already in the Finlay market, vying busily for custom.

Holmes and I followed Philomel over the cobbled streets of the Lower Town, descending to the level of the St. Lawrence. The tide was moving upstream against the river torrent, creating whirlpools and eddies in its wake. Philomel, a loquacious man in his forties, spoke in a rapid *patois* which I could barely follow, save to realize that he was professing pride in the shipbuilding capabilities of Quebec past and present. Holmes seemed to find no difficulty in carrying on a lively conversation with him.

"One must understand," cried Philomel, "on the banks of the St. Lawrence at Quebec for two hundred years, we have built fine ships to sail the world. Ships of wood, that are propelled by the wind. And now we can build ships of iron that go by steam."

"You can build the engines for the steamships?" asked Holmes.

"Ah, yes, m'sieur. Everything. We fabricate the steel and the bronze. We have the machine shops and the skilled workers in metal."

Under Philomel's guidance we had entered a shipyard. The door of a blast furnace swung open and revealed a searing white heart of brilliant heat and light, before which the flesh cringed and the eye averted itself. A stream of molten metal flowed from a glowing crucible, spitting white-hot incandescence into a cigar-shaped mold.

"Bronze, m'sieur," shouted Philomel, above the roar of the furnace.

"For what?"

"Part of a vessel, m'sieur."

"There is a machine shop also, you said."

"More than one. Well equipped, one can imagine."

Two men, muffled in heavy aprons, leather gloves and goggles against the heat, moved the giant ladle on a counterbalanced system of pulleys and finished pouring the mold. A third man was supervising the operation. It was only when the molten white-hot stream stopped flowing that he noticed our presence. His head came sharply around and he shouted angrily at our companion, projecting his voice above the furnace's roar. Although I did not understand his words, his meaning was clear. We were not supposed to be there. Philomel remonstrated, shouting and waving his arms at the supervisor, then turned to us.

"Pardon, messieurs, Jean-Baptiste objects to our presence. He threatens to make trouble. We must go."

"Yes, of course," replied Holmes, "then let us go. Perhaps he thinks we are in danger from the furnace."

"Yes, m'sieur, perhaps that is it."

We retreated from the heat and noise of the foundry.

"Jean-Baptiste, he has many good songs of the river, that one," said Philomel, disappointment in his voice. "In other circumstances you would like him, messieurs."

Holmes had some business of his own to attend to, and I was happy to stroll on my own and delight in the fresh spring morning and the friendly demeanour and independent air of the *québecois* going about their business. I made some inquiries at the Bureau of Navigation, to check charts of the river and the tide tables. I was intrigued by my findings. It was almost with reluctance that I returned to the inn through the sunny streets.

Our host, a grizzled Frenchman of some fifty years, was not to be seen. Neither was the landlady, nor Holmes. I went up to our rooms and tapped on the latter's door.

"*Entrez.*"

I opened the door and found Holmes seated at his small table, going over some papers. I closed the door behind me.

"The Tides of Spring," I said abruptly.

"Yes?"

"I checked with the Navigation Bureau. Charts, tide tables and so on."

"Was it useful?"

"I think so." He poured me a glass of sherry. "The height of the tides at any given moment in the River St. Lawrence varies in the five hundred miles between the sea and the port of Quebec, depending upon many factors I need not enumerate." I sipped the sherry gratefully. "But they have been charted and are predictable," I went on. Holmes leaned back in his chair and closed his eyes, listening in his singular meditative way.

I continued: "The next spring tide will occur when the moon is full. The tides will then be at their highest for the month of May, again varying in the length of the river. There is one point the night of the full moon at which the spring tide will stand at twenty-one feet."

". . . at Quebec for two hundred years, we have built fine ships to sail the world . . ."

"*Vingt-et-un*," murmured Holmes."

"Exactly."

I spread a section of the navigation chart for the River St. Lawrence on his table, and I put my finger on a particular fiord-like inlet.

"The Saguenay," I said.

There was a pause. Holmes's eyes opened and his long arm reached for his notebook. He found the appropriate entry, and read aloud: "'Maxim on board ship, under cover of darkness, speaks to crew member, not identified. Vulgar phrase in local French, reference to '*le roi*,' laughter, something changes hands, '*au Saguenay*' — "

"Maxim," I exclaimed. "Surely he is not part of a foul plot — "

"Not knowingly, perhaps," replied Holmes grimly.

"Ha ha," I went on.

"What?" said Holmes.

"Your brother Mycroft's cryptic utterance in his cable. 'Ha ha.'"

"What about it?"

"It is a place, Holmes. Deep within the fiord." I pointed at the chart. "Baie de Ha Ha. Remote, uninhabited. The chart shows a depth of 1,400 feet, and the cliffs rise sheer from the water a similar distance into the air, obscuring the sun. The Indians consider it the abode of evil spirits, according to the garrulous fellow who sold me this chart."

"What significance would your spring tides have in waters of such great depth?"

"I can't think — unless there is shoal water that would be a danger to navigation. Perhaps the time of the spring tide is used simply as a way to synchronize movements. I have the tide tables here — "

Holmes had snatched up Mycroft's cable.

"Bertie gone ahunting . . . ha ha . . . cows. Cowes? Watson, I believe that my brother Mycroft, with the flippancy to which he occasionally descends, is using the name 'Bertie' to refer to no less august a personage than the Prince of Wales, who would doubtless embark from Cowes if he were to make a nautical journey. Don't sailors generally leave port at first light?"

"It is quite usual, Holmes, in these days of steam."

"How long would it take the royal yacht *Alexandra*, or perhaps the *Victoria and Albert*, to steam from Cowes to the Saguenay? Ten days?"

"I should think so."

"And when is your next spring tide?"

"In ten days."

Holmes's grey eyes shone with suppressed excitement. "Well, then, we have a *rendez-vous* of immense importance, ten days hence, in the deep dark waters of the Saguenay. Well done, Watson!"

At this moment there was a light footstep on the stair, and a hurried knock came at the door. As Holmes swept away his papers and pocketed his notebook, I concealed my chart.

"*Entrez,*" Holmes called.

The door opened. There stood Madeleine de Vernisse, poised and elegant as ever, but with a flush on her cheek that betokened considerable agitation.

"Madame," Holmes rose from his chair. "I am honoured. Please sit down." He removed a litter of Quebec and Montreal newspapers from the modest divan with which his room was equipped. She swirled her fashionable skirts and sat, wasting not a moment in small talk.

"Hiram Maxim has gone!" she said.

"Gone, madame?" Holmes concealed his surprise, but from under half-closed lids his sharp eyes surveyed our visitor.

"I will be frank with you, Monsieur Holmes."

"You know my identity, then."

"I do. And I know that you are employed by the British Government to shadow Monsieur Maxim, to see that he does not get into trouble in America, so that finally he will return to London with a new and improved version of his M-gun, and whatever else he may have invented in the meantime."

"You are well informed, madame."

"I am, m'sieur. In my travels I meet many people of rank, highly placed and powerful, people who inform me. The stakes are high, m'sieur. Many people would like to have the M-gun. You have lost Monsieur Maxim. You must find him again."

"You didn't find him at the shipyard, then?"

"M'sieur?" Her eyes flashed at him, suddenly alert.

"Madame!" Holmes's voice crackled with barely controlled irritation. "You enter my rooms hurriedly, your usual composure not quite intact. Although you arrived here in a dogcart, which you dismissed at the door, there are vestiges of clay on the heel and side of your boot which could have only come from the shipyard, or more precisely from the floor of the foundry at the Pointe Diamante shipyard. And your usual delicate perfume, madame, if I may say so, is somewhat spoiled by the distinctive sharp sulphurous odour of molten bronze which has clung to your clothing and hair, as you undoubtedly rushed directly here from the shipyard, rather than going first to your own abode."

"Bravo, M'sieur Holmes," she cried, clapping her gloved hands in gentle mockery.

Holmes was not put off by her raillery. "Why the haste, madame? Why the agitation? Is it only the disappearance of Monsieur Maxim?"

"M'sieur," she said at last, "I must tell you all. You will find out soon enough."

"Do so, madame, if you please. Otherwise I cannot help you."

"I came here directly, as you say, to seek your help, because there has been a tragic accident in the foundry at Pointe Diamante. Barely an hour ago, a stream of molten metal engulfed and took the life of Philomel Leblanc."

Philomel! That open generous fellow, whose innocence had met such a desperate end!

"I am deeply distressed," said Holmes. "We were with him earlier today. It was an accident, you say, madame?"

"I am assured it was, m'sieur. But one is aware of so many dark places in the human heart!"

"You are linking this sad event with the disappearance of Monsieur Maxim?"

"Let us say there is a coincidence in time only, m'sieur; I have known Hiram Maxim for many years, but in the final analysis how well does one ever know the inner heart of one's fellow being?"

"And Philomel? How is it that a lady of your station finds herself in the noise and dirt of an iron foundry? What is Philomel to you?"

At Holmes's words, Madame de Vernisse turned pale. She rose and fixed her tormentor with a cold, level gaze, and her voice was scathing.

"Understand, sir, I am the last of a line of *seigneurs* that goes back to the beginnings of the French settlement of North America. Philomel Leblanc was as precious to me as any member of this proud community."

Holmes got swiftly to his feet, reaching out his hand. "Forgive me, madame," he said. "I did not wish to offend. Please do not distress yourself — "

She looked him in the eyes, her breath coming quickly, and I wondered whether what I saw between them was just a figment of the imagination that Holmes affected to despise.

"Perhaps a glass of sherry?" he asked.

"Thank you, m'sieur, that would be welcome." Her voice was low, and it trembled slightly. She composed herself and sat

"... a man's life ..."

again on the divan. Holmes poured a glass of sherry from the decanter, and gave it to her. As she sipped, the colour returned to her cheeks.

"As you put it so well, madame, we are charged to see that Monsieur Maxim does not get into trouble in America. Perhaps you could confide in us, and tell us what sort of trouble he may be in."

"I cannot tell you precisely, Mr. Holmes. We have our private lives, after all. But as always, when he is restless, he may disappear in the wilderness for many days or weeks. He does not change, m'sieur."

"How does he disappear, madame?"

"In the old days, when we were both much younger, it would be by canoe, exploring the deep rivers and the great cataracts."

"And now?"

"You heard him speak with such enthusiasm of his underwater experiments?"

"He said, if I remember aright, that he was thinking about something of the sort."

"*Non, mon Dieu*, it has gone far beyond thought. With Maxim, to think is to act!"

"Are you saying that Maxim has an operable submarine vessel?"

"It is what he calls a submersible, built to his designs, in secret, here in Quebec. For whom, and with what funds, I do not know. But I fear for him."

"Why?"

"Because at heart he remains a simple, vulnerable boy playing with his toys. After a lifetime of achievement and success in the real world, he is still capable of foolish, thoughtless, grandiose action. I can say no more than that." Her voice trembled with emotion, and she dabbed at her eyes with a delicate lace handkerchief.

Holmes remained silent, and after a moment our visitor regained her composure. As she rose to take her departure, the tears were gone, and when she spoke again, her voice was controlled and vibrant.

"Gentlemen, you must find Maxim. It is of extreme importance."

I opened the door for her, and she swept past me. We heard her light step on the stairs.

That night I did not fall into my usual, untroubled sleep. My head whirled with disturbing images. The beautiful, distressed face of Madeleine de Vernisse became the stained, weeping Queen of Diamonds, which was then overlaid by the golden image of the voracious Chien d'Or, gnawing its human thighbone. I dreamed of Maxim as I had first seen him in the underground firing-range in London, his nimbus of white hair flaring in the light of the acetylene torches. His words echoed in my head, as if from stone walls: "I have a weapon which will change the fortunes of the nation that possesses it." Holmes's voice hissed in my ear, "The Mark of the Beast!" and from the walls of the lady's elegant dining room boomed Maxim's voice: "Consider, gentlemen, an airborne fleet, able to rain death down from on high."

I awakened abruptly, and started up, my heart thumping wildly. I stared about, but all was silent. Through my casement window, serenely illuminating a sleeping world, I saw the half-grown moon sailing aloft, brilliant, untouched, unsullied, unaware of the turbulent currents in the tides of Earth and the affairs of men.

There was a pitcher of water beside the bed. I drank from it feverishly, and my heart returned to normal. I threw off my coverlet and crossed to the window, flinging the casement wide to the cool night air. Below me, under the moon's pale gaze, flowed the St. Lawrence, smooth and silent. My ugly dreams were dispelled, soothed as always by the flow of the river's eternal stream.

Then, as I watched, I became aware of a movement, a slight turbulence on the smooth surface: a dark shape, where a moment before there had been but open water. I thought perhaps it was a whale, that most magnificent of the creatures of the water, venturing far from its home in the sea. As I reached for my binoculars and focussed on the object, it emerged from the water; the magnifying lenses brought it close to my eye, sharply defined, its wet surfaces glinting in the moonlight.

I gasped. I was looking at a submarine. Low and wicked, fully sixty feet in length, it surged on the surface of the river heading upstream, picking up speed. In its passage it left behind a turbulent wake, from which issued smoke and white steam. On the quiet night air I could faintly hear the throb of engines.

I turned from the window and, pulling on a dressing gown, went at once to Holmes's room. I tapped quietly on the door, and spoke in an urgent whisper.

"Holmes!"

There was no response. I turned the knob and opened the door. From the river, a sudden gust of cold air blew wide the casements, and the room was flooded with moonlight. The bed was empty. The sheets were crumpled and awry, and to my touch they felt cold. I looked about for signs of a struggle, or for a note he might have left me, but there was nothing. His outdoor clothing had gone, and so had Holmes.

# Chapter XIII
# A Life Is in Danger

In my years of association with Sherlock Holmes I had grown used to his abrupt disappearances. He would vanish for days at a time into the vast underworld of London, where he maintained, I believe, a number of lodgings and as many disguises and contacts to assist him in investigative work. Then one day he would as suddenly reappear in our Baker Street rooms in the role of a bookseller, a bearded sea captain, or perhaps a common tout, and fling off his disguise with a boyish and triumphant laugh, ready to tell of the most recent development in whatever case he was working on. I found him once in a foul opium den, in one of London's most disreputable districts.

So I waited patiently for a day or so in our Quebec lodgings, putting my notes up to date and hoping to hear from him. The second day I climbed Breakneck Stairs, the shortest route from Lower Town's Champlain Street to the Rue de Buade, where I thought to seek the advice of Madame de Vernisse. But upon locating her château and braving the baleful Chien d'Or, my trip proved fruitless. After I had spent some minutes knocking on the great door, the aged servitor answered my summons, but to my inquiry for Madame de Vernisse, he responded only that Madame was *pas ici*, and he didn't know where she had gone or when she would return. With which, he bade me good day and closed the heavy door.

I descended again to the Lower Town, my heart full of foreboding. At the inn at this time of day, the parlour was empty, and I was about to ascend to my room, when under the stairs a small door swung ajar. I paused, and had to crane over the banisters to see the cause of this action. Half in and half out of the opening was the little laughing pig I had seen previously. He looked up at me, grinning. Through the partly open door came the smell of tobacco smoke, and the murmur of male voices in subdued conversation. On an impulse I turned and followed the little pink pig, and found myself in a dark passageway cut into the face of the rock. The animal nosed opened another door, and I entered a small low-ceilinged room, lit by a lantern and a guttering candle. Around a pine table, smoking clay pipes, sat three men who wore the tuques and sashes of the shantymen, the men of the forest and the river. One was an older version of Philomel, that decent man of music, whose life had been so cruelly shortened. The second, a slender, saturnine fellow in his forties, seemed oddly familiar to my eye, but somehow out of context here, in this setting. The third man's aquiline nose, his high cheek bones and bronze skin, betrayed his Indian origins. I recalled Holmes's dissertations on the subject of racial anatomy, and wished anew that my friend were at hand to advise me.

A chair was pushed in my direction, "Watson, do sit down!" The voice came from the Indian. I sat down abruptly, stunned once again by the unexpected presence of Sherlock Holmes.

"This is François Leblanc. He works in the machine shop. He is the older brother of Philomel," said Holmes. The little pig was nuzzling François's calloused hand, and for his pains received half a winter apple.

"My deep sympathy, M'sieur François," said I.

"That man over there is Louis Frechette. He was an assistant engineer on your ship."

"M'sieur," the dark slender man nodded to me.

First assistant engineer! Now I placed him. He was the fellow Maxim had spoken to, that dark night on the boat deck of the *Etruria*. Holmes was now talking to the other two men in French, seeming already to have picked up the nasal tones of the Quebec *patois*.

"Watson, these men tell me that Maxim has indeed been developing a submersible here, with the excellent craftsmen available to him working to his designs."

"In this yard, in '33, we built the first steamship for the ocean crossing, the *Royal William*," François interjected with a note of pride.

"Exactly," said Holmes. "The workmanship is not in doubt, it is of the finest. But mark this, Watson: Maxim's packing cases, which we followed across the Atlantic, contain not the M-gun as we surmised, but elements for the submersible devised in Britain. The vessel has now had secret test runs in the St. Lawrence."

"I saw it the night before last, Holmes, through my binoculars. It surfaced, and proceeded at what appeared to be about twelve knots."

"A trifle faster than that, actually. It is sixty-four feet in length, and powered by steam turbines while on the surface. The turbines generate electrical energy which is stored in accumulator batteries for underwater passage. It is equipped with two Whitehead torpedoes, driven by compressed air, each of which, when armed, carries a hundred and twenty pounds of dynamite in its nose."

"An awesome weapon."

"A cut above Nordenfeldt's crude prototype," Holmes agreed.

"On whose authority is this undertaken?" I asked.

"Whose, indeed! These matters are cloaked in secrecy, supposedly in the national interest." Holmes was acerbic. "One is never quite sure who knows what and who supports whom. Whitehead, an Englishman, builds torpedoes in Fiume. Holland, the fellow in the States, builds a submersible for the Fenians to attack British shipping. Maxim, an American, chooses to work in Britain, and apparently under cover here in Quebec."

"M'sieurs," François broke in. "I am not concerned, me, with national interests, or the secrecy of inventions, but with the death of my brother. It was not an accident, that death. Whatever Monsieur Maxim intended with his incredible machine, a weapon to protect, to defend, it is now a thing of horror. I, Philomel, our father, our grandfathers, worked with pride in these shipyards, in this country. Now, the remains of Philomel lie in his coffin, defaced beyond recognition, the result of a deliberate, horrible murder." The good François buried his face in his hands.

Through all this, the other fellow had sat silent, puffing his pipe, listening. Holmes turned to him. "And you, Louis Frechette?"

Frechette blew a cloud of smoke. "M'sieur, I am a marine engineer. I know very well the type of engine with which the vessel of Monsieur Maxim is equipped — the condensers and the accumulators. Also, I am most familiar with the river, the channels and currents and sand banks which one must negotiate a hundred and twenty miles between Quebec and the River of the Saguenay."

"Again the Saguenay!" said Holmes.

"*Oui*, m'sieur. It was the intention of Monsieur Maxim to navigate the submersible to the Saguenay, for some demonstration in those deep waters."

"Where is Monsieur Maxim now?"

"Ah, that is the great mystery. Every day for a week he was at the yard, exclaiming with great pleasure at the work, installing the equipment he brought from England, finally taking the vessel on its trials."

"And now?"

Louis gave a Gallic shrug, "You understand, m'sieur, one man does not build a vessel like this. There are many experts. One designer, perhaps, a genius like Monsieur Maxim, but then many specialists."

"In the shops are bosses we have not seen before," said François. "The good feeling is gone."

"Something is wrong, messieurs. That is why we are here talking to you."

". . . Holland . . . builds a submersible . . ."

Holmes was refuelling his pipe with the Canadian tobacco he had come to favour. In a moment he spoke again: "Why the Saguenay?"

"M'sieur?"

"The Saguenay," repeated Holmes, "is a hundred and twenty miles downstream through sand bars and river currents, you tell me."

"A *rendez-vous*," said Louis Frechette.

"With whom?"

"With a ship. A very important meeting, Monsieur Maxim said. He would rub his hands together with pleasure when he mentioned it."

"You know him well, Monsieur Maxim?"

"Oh, *oui*, m'sieur. As young men we were like brothers together on these waters. Rafting, chasing girls, getting into the fist fights." At the memory, Frechette winked at his comrade, who responded with a grin, his mood lifting. "Those were the days there, eh, François?"

"For sure," replied François. He reached into a cupboard, from which he took glasses and a dark green bottle. "Whisky *blanc*," he said, and applied his energy to withdrawing the cork. Holmes exhaled a cloud of smoke.

"And Madame de Vernisse?" he asked.

François glanced up, "Madame la Madeleine, eh?" The cork came out of the whisky bottle with a pop. He carefully poured the drinks and replaced the cork in the bottle. Then he blew on his fingers, as if they were hot. "*Ouf*, let us say, Madame de Vernisse she lives in a world of her own, that one!" He banged in the cork with the heel of his hand. "Down the 'atch, messieurs!"

We gulped down the fiery liquid.

"Ouf! *Ça va!*"

"Truly," said Holmes in a hoarse voice.

Holmes again addressed Louis Frechette, "Time of the *rendez-vous*?"

"In four days, at the height of the tide."

"Spring tide."

"Correct, *ça*."

"Time of departure?"

"From here, m'sieur, tomorrow night at the ebb."

"Is there any way in which we could get on board the submersible?"

"M'sieur, it is a magnificent vessel for the engines and boilers, the generators and accumulators, and the storage of fuel and water, but for human beings the accommodation is small. There is room only for a few persons. The engineer, the firemen, the commander and the second officer, and all these of course are specialists. Also they must do double duty. Seven persons at the most."

I interjected for the first time: "But if, as you say, there is trouble, and a man has already lost his life, should the boat be allowed to leave port?"

"You cannot stop it, m'sieur. The authorities say Philomel's death was an accident. There are strong forces at work here, things beyond my comprehension."

"We have no authority, Watson," snapped Holmes.

"But Holmes, if, as you fear — "

"My dear Watson," interrupted Holmes. "No matter what I may fear, it is necessary to follow this affair to the end."

Our two French companions gazed at us puzzled — unable, perhaps, to follow our rapid English speech; I was not entirely clear myself what Holmes had in mind.

"We must take it that it is the wish and intention of the Prince of Wales to attend the demonstration of this submersible in the privacy of the Saguenay," Holmes continued. "It is possible that he authorized the project himself, after viewing the limitations of the Nordenfeldt submarine at Lanskrona."

"But if your assessment of Wilkins's message is correct — "

" — and the very life of the Prince is in danger?"

"Exactly, Holmes!"

"Then we have a nice problem, Watson. Brother Mycroft would be most put out if the Prince were to arrive only to discover that the performance had been called off."

"But Holmes — "

"On the other hand, we cannot allow these miscreants the freedom to carry out their designs, if indeed such deeds are contemplated. It is a very nice problem." His blackened clay pipe had gone out, and he set about relighting it.

"Holmes," I cried, "You are prepared to gamble — "

"Let us not forget that Her Majesty's Diamond Jubilee celebrations are imminent, bringing a terrifying opportunity to shake the Empire. Should these desperadoes succeed, the deed would encourage others of like mind. The principals in this case remain elusive, Watson." In Holmes's lean fingers a vesta match suddenly flared, and he applied the flame to his pipe bowl. "I know who they are and what they intend to do, and when and where. But the trap must be set." He blew out a cloud of smoke, and extinguished the match. "That is why I must get aboard the vessel."

"M'sieur," François Leblanc spoke up. His brow was dark. "I could not understand your English words. All I know is that I want to come face to face with the one who took my brother's life."

"Can you get us on board the submersible, François?" asked Holmes.

"I can try, m'sieur, but it would be dangerous if you are recognized."

"We can but try," said Holmes. "Are you game, Watson?" There was suppressed excitement in his voice.

"As always," I replied.


It proved not so difficult after all. At a prearranged hour after dark, the tide still two hours short of the ebb, a small lighter delivered provisions to the submersible, which, concealed under a shed roof, was lying comfortably alongside a floating dock. Among the three or four dockyard hands who passed the goods on board were Holmes and myself, dressed in borrowed clothes shabby enough to pass muster. With us was François Leblanc, brother of the dead Philomel. Louis Frechette, in his capacity as engineer, was already on board, preparing for the coming voyage. We heard a dynamo humming somewhere below, and electric light shone from ports in the conning tower and from the open hatches through which we passed the provisions for the voyage. This light glinted on the dark water of the river as it lapped against the metal skin of the vessel, but did little to dispel the blackness of the overcast night which pressed in upon us. The gleaming surface of the submarine stretched into the gloom at either end of its considerable length, its details lost in darkness. This much I observed while passing up boxes of bully beef and sacks of onions.

The hatches had limited capacity to take all we handed up from the lighter, so that the deck quickly became littered. Only one fellow stood on the submersible's deck; another, down below, was presumably handing the stuff into the vessel's galley and storage spaces.

Holmes took in the situation and hesitated not a moment, but with his usual agility clambered from the deck of the lighter to that of the submersible. The fellow in the hatch had vanished below, and Holmes replaced him.

"*Allons-y*! Give a hand, eh?" François shouted at me, pointing to the deck of the underwater craft. As smartly as I could, considering my old war wound, I followed his order, and was soon handing the provisions from the deck to Holmes in the hatchway.

A moment later Holmes vanished below with a sack of potatoes and I was considering whether to take his place when I became aware of a steam launch approaching out of the darkness of the river, shooting sparks from its smokestack. As it came to rest alongside the lighter, a line was passed across. The man handling the launch was Jean-Baptiste, whom I had seen in the smelter supervising the pouring of the molten bronze and berating the good Philomel for our presence. He shouted at François in the same arrogant manner: "Isn't that stuff all on board yet?"

"The last is going below now," François replied with restraint.

From within the cabin of the launch appeared a steward, carrying a number of bulky packages, who clambered across the deck of the lighter and into the submarine. Then a bigger man appeared, a figure of authority in a serviceable pea jacket and marine officer's cap, carrying a dunnage bag under one arm. Silhouetted against the dim light from the cabin, he stood for a moment, running a practised eye over the vessel before him. Then he spoke in good European French.

"Jean-Baptiste."

"M'sieur?"

"Report to me in person, when all is secure. In half an hour we raise steam, and single up. We go with the ebb."

"*Oui, m'sieur le capitaine,*" responded Jean-Baptiste, touching his cap.

The newcomer climbed aboard the submersible with every sign of familiarity. It was only when he swung himself into the open hatch of the conning tower, that the light from below caught his face, and I saw who it was. "*M'sieur le capitaine*" was the Baron von Kramm!

At the sight of the Baron, any doubts I might have entertained about Wilkins's cryptic "message of the cards" were swept away. As he stood there for a moment, lit from below like a figure on a stage, I gazed at that rakish countenance. I saw for the first time his facial scars — the sabre cuts which betokened the rigorous German military officer-training of an elite group. Professional adventurer, gambler, man of the world, he was the classic *agent provocateur*, moving in high places, a man whose actions on behalf of his employer could shape history. This was our adversary. He took a last look around, then went below and was lost to my sight.

The remainder of the provisions had been passed below through the forward hatch, and in a moment I was joined by Sherlock Holmes.

"I have the information I need, Watson." He spoke urgently, close to my ear. "My plans are laid. *Rendez-vous au Saguenay! Au 'voir.*"

Before I could respond he had clambered aboard the lighter, which was shoving off. The steam launch stood by. I gazed about me in despair, standing on the deck of this extraordinary vessel a few feet above the dark waters of the St. Lawrence. As I have said, the submarine measured sixty-odd feet in length by about nine feet in beam at its broadest point, tapering like a monstrous metal cigar at both ends. Before and abaft the conning tower, a small deck was rivetted to the upper surface of the boat for a foothold, and something of a handrail provided some protection against sliding overboard. A man's head appeared at the after hatch.

"Jean!" he barked in French. "Yes, you there. Get below. You are my new fireman! Jump to it!"

It was Louis Frechette, the engineer in charge, and it was me he was shouting at. Holmes had indeed laid his plans. I hoped I would live through them.

# Chapter XIV
# "What Are You Doing in My Ship?"

In my time I have spent some years in ships, even beating around the Horn in one of the last great grain clippers, but never had I experienced anything like this. To be cooped up in a space no larger than a sewer pipe, a space, furthermore, that was already as full as human ingenuity could devise, with control mechanisms, steering gear links and cables which ran fore and aft through iron bulkheads, containers of compressed air, pressure pumps, water pumps, ballast tanks, generators, accumulators, and the marvelously contrived steam engine that drove the whole extraordinary vessel — to find myself inside this monster induced in me a feeling of being trapped just as surely as Holmes's rats on board the *Etruria* had been. I strove to forget the unfortunate image.

On the surface, under steam, we cruised at a good ten knots. The vessel appeared to handle not too differently from any other modern steamship, the officer in command passing his orders from conning tower to helmsman and engine room through a voice pipe. It was also possible for the officer to con the ship from a position directly beside the helmsman, watching his passage through portholes.

As Louis Frechette had said, one did double duty on board the submersible, and so a few hours after casting off, I found myself called from the engine room to relieve the man at the wheel. In my square-rig days I had spent long stints steering by compass or stars under the Southern Cross, so I took over the wheel with quickly returning confidence, peering at the compass card which swung in gimbals before me, and at once calling out the course to the officer — the Baron himself was conning the vessel. It was only after I had so confidently and automatically sounded off, that I realized I had spoken in English.

The Baron was peering ahead through night glasses. At my voice, he lowered the glasses and turned to look at me.

"English," he said.

"Irish, sorr," I responded.

His eyes flickered in what appeared to be slight amusement. He lifted the glasses again.

"Port a bit," he said.

"Port a bit, sorr." I swung the wheel.

"Steady on nor'-east by a point east."

I met the swing of the vessel and steadied on the new course. I sang out the new heading.

"Very good," he said, and marked our position on the chart by the dim light from the binnacle. "And what are you doing in my ship, Irishman? I have not seen you before."

"I replaced one of the firemen, sorr. His wife took sick, sorr."

"These soft, *verdammt* Frenchmen," he said quietly. He marked course and speed and checked the chronometer.

"Yes, sorr."

"Not like the Germans. Or the Irish."

"*No*, sorr."

He finished his precise chart-work, and turned to me. "So what are you doing in my ship?" he repeated. I noted that he did not mention Maxim, whose ship I presumed the submersible to be.

Some of Holmes's words flashed into my head: "When in doubt, tell the truth."

"Spying," said I.

The Baron looked at me with mild amusement, surprised no doubt at my audacity. I plunged on, embroidering the truth.

"I am a Fenian, sorr. From the States. As you may know, sorr, we have been raising funds in New York and Chicago to build submersibles with which to attack British ships. We would put them on board freighters bound for British ports, and seek out the ships of the Royal Navy wherever we found them."

"Holland." The glasses had gone back to his eyes as he surveyed the channel ahead.

"Sorr?"

"The designer. John Holland, Irish-American, hates the British. Built his boats on the Hudson River. Not practical. Watch your course, helmsman."

"Aye, aye, sir." I adjusted the wheel. "Course steady on nor'-east by a point east."

"Very good." The Baron was silent for some moments, and I heard only the steady throb of the steam engines and the sound of the river's turbulence past our slender hull.

"Irishman, what do you hope to spy out on my ship?" he queried finally.

"I hope perhaps, sorr, to help strike a blow for old Ireland," I volunteered.

"In my ship?" His voice had hardened, and panic suddenly rose in my throat. I wasn't supposed to know the evil purpose of this voyage.

"As a loyal Irishman, sorr, wherever and whenever." I tried to get an element of stubborn, loyal stupidity into my voice.

He looked at me for a moment, intently. Then the binoculars went back to his eyes, and he surveyed the watery path ahead, shining in the light of the full moon which had now appeared from behind a bank of cloud.

"The Rising of the Moon," he said.

"Sorr?"

"Don't you Irish have a song?"

"We do that, sorr," I replied, wondering what song he had in mind.

"A thousand pikes will glitter, in the rising of the moon," he recited.

"That's it, sorr," said I.

The Baron paused, "Irishman," he said.

"Sorr."

"You are a good helmsman."

"Thank you, sorr."

"And if you are what you say you are, I promise you, I will shortly give you a chance to strike a blow for Ireland. If you are not — " He lowered the binoculars, and stared at me. The look in his eyes chilled my heart.

I was relieved at eight bells — four o'clock in the morning. Armed with a hot cup of strong sweet tea, I gratefully escaped the enclosed space and sought the freedom of the upper deck. The May air was balmy, scented with pine and spruce and the ever-present undefinable river smell. Our craft was making good time, surging downstream over the dark moonlit waters as if in a dream. Navigation lights were rare, and only pine trees stuck in the bottom marked the presence of sand bars — marks easy to miss for a person unfamiliar with these waters. The job of river pilot was a hereditary one, handed down from father to son, and jealously guarded, but men like Louis Frechette and presumably Jean-Baptiste knew the waters from long acquaintance, and we were well within the channel.

I found Louis in the lee of the conning tower, taking his ease with a pipe. We sat together on the tiny deck, the dark river surging past just below our feet, nothing between us and eternity but a slender guardrail. I lit my pipe as he spoke in a low voice.

"I was there in the foundry when Philomel died, m'sieur. I must tell you. That man there, the Commander, was present. And with him — Madame de Vernisse."

At this disclosure I started, and clung to my frail perch.

"I see you are dismayed, m'sieur. But more transpired. My good old friend and companion of the river, Monsieur Maxim, appeared. He was very excited and angry at finding these two together. You understand that Madeleine was Maxim's woman since many years. There was a fight. Imagine, m'sieur, the roaring of the furnaces, the great ladle of molten bronze ready to pour into the molds. And these two big men fighting over the hand of *la petite Madeleine*. Such a fight. Fists and feet, like men from the lumber camp. And the lady watching, her bosom heaving, her dark eyes glittering. What a woman to fight for!"

"And Philomel?" I asked.

"I think Philomel tried to intercede. But the ladle was tipping, and he was in the way of the molten metal. Too late Maxim tried to help, and while he was diverted, the Commander there felled him with a tremendous blow. All was madness, you understand, m'sieur, in smoke and fumes and shouting. Jean-Baptiste was in charge of the smelter pouring operation. He ordered me out *et me fermer ma bouche là*. That is the last I saw."

"What happened to Maxim?"

"I am sorry, m'sieur, that is all I know. Now you know it also."

"And now?"

"Now, I carry through Monsieur Maxim's wishes, to *rendez-vous* with the other vessel."

"Under the command of the man who tried to destroy Monsieur Maxim?" I cried, horrified.

"They were partners, m'sieur."

"But surely — "

"*Enfin*, I am a simple man. I have my instructions, m'sieur, and I shall carry them out to the best of my ability." Louis Frechette, excusing himself, made his way back to the after hatch and squeezed himself below through that narrow opening. Another pawn in Holmes's dangerous game, I thought.

The submersible ran into an area of turbulence in the dark river, and with our low freeboard, a heavy wave rolled over the deck. It occurred to me that whatever its underwater capabilities, on the surface this vessel would be singularly vulnerable to any kind of heavy sea. With the hatches open, as they were at present, we could flood and sink like a stone.

I caught a few hours' sleep in a narrow bunk, cramped into the after part of the vessel adjacent to the engine room, before being called again to the backbreaking task of raking ashes and shovelling coal. While we were on the surface, the after hatch provided ventilation for the engine room and a means of disposal for burned fuel. We had not yet dived. I gathered that this was a delicate procedure, entailing closing down the steam engine and switching to electrical drive from the accumulators, and breathing

". . . the royal yacht *Victoria and Albert* . . ."

air and oxygen compressed in bottles for the purpose. I did not look forward to this experience.

When I had the ashes hauled and new coals ablaze, and observed that the steam gauges were at the correct reading, I stuck my head out of the after hatch for a breath of air. The sun was just rising ahead of us on the starboard bow, emerging glowing pink from behind a distant fog bank. The St. Lawrence at this point had widened greatly, but we hugged the channel of the North Shore. A few farms of cleared land shewed pale green with spring growth amidst the dark forest, running back from the river. Peaceful ribbons of white smoke rose into the still air from neat stone houses, with their characteristically steep roof lines, as stoves were lighted for the morning meal. An Indian canoe with two occupants glided silent as a ghost between us and the shore, close in under the land. In the light of early morning I could now see, one on either side of the vessel, outlined against our bow wave, the tubes that held the deadly Whitehead torpedoes.

Only then did I fully realize, as I stood in the cool clean perfume of the morning air, a mote in the midst of God's glorious firmament, that my own efforts were helping this evil instrument of destruction on its deadly mission to assassinate the future King. For I had no doubt now what was afoot. What Maxim had originally intended, I did not know. Perhaps the vessel that moved so smoothly beneath me was truly intended to serve Her Majesty, perhaps it was the first of many to defend the Empire against those who would destroy it. Perhaps the Prince of Wales had been legitimately invited to view the manoeuvers and firepower of the Maxim submersible in the deep lonely waters of the Saguenay, much as he had inspected the Nordenfeldt ship in Landskrona. But this time the visit was secret. "Gone ahunting," Mycroft had said. Such, at least, was Holmes's theory.

But I knew at that moment that beyond the rosy dawn, miles to the east, the royal yacht *Victoria and Albert* was speeding innocently to her death in the remote, silent Saguenay. If she were to be blasted out of the water by a dastardly torpedo attack, the explosion would be heard around the world. Headlines would flare in the newspapers, blaming the Fenians, their American supporters, and the Riel faction in Canada. International recriminations would follow, "Manifest Destiny" again be cried, navies strengthened; new and more efficient engines of destruction would be developed. And the Baron von Kramm, the classic *agent provocateur*, would melt again into the murky pool of international espionage.

Did Holmes know the facts surrounding Philomel's death in the awful fiery cauldron of the foundry, the explosion of jealous rage between von Kramm and Maxim, the fateful, fatal part played by Madeleine de Vernisse? My mind held the image of her in our rooms at the inn, announcing the death of Philomel — the beautiful face, flushed and concerned, the trembling voice, the hint of tears, the delicate lace handkerchief. A most persuasive performance, I thought bitterly. Had my friend Homes again been outwitted by a woman?

I was called below by the harsh voice of Jean-Baptiste. In the limited, noisy space of the engine room, he gave me a tongue-lashing, shouting obscenities, berating me for neglecting the fires. I do not take insults kindly, and my fists bunched at his foul words. I have a violent temper when aroused, and have on occasion plunged into a fight without thought for the consequences. He grinned at my response and moved, lithe as a whip, hands open, ready to strike or to grip. "*Allons-y, mon vieux*," he said, beckoning me towards him.

It was well that at that moment Jean Frechette entered the engine compartment, saw the situation at a glance and defused it, making some disparaging remark about the "*sacré* Irish." He then turned on me with an oath and got me to stoking his confounded fires again. Jean-Baptiste sneered at me and spat on the floor before he swung through the communicating watertight door and left us.

"*Bâtard!*" exclaimed Jean Frechette. "His time will come, m'sieur, I promise you!"

My hands blistered with the unaccustomed work, my heart labouring in the heat of the engine room, I wiped the sweat out of my eyes with a dirty forearm. I grinned to myself: I had two promises in one day, and the day was hardly yet begun.

# Chapter XV
# The Frightful Affair
# in the Baie de Ha Ha

It was noon by the time we drew abreast of the entrance to the Saguenay, a mile or so offshore. It was marked by the village of Tadoussac, the earliest white habitation on the North American continent. A slender church spire dominated the settlement, gleaming in the light of the sun, now at its zenith in the cloudless sky. Behind the village, in muted tones of violet and grey, lay the ancient humped hills of the Laurentians. Closer to the river, dark green woods were broken by massive outcroppings of granite. Along the shoreline, seeking the countercurrent, moved a log raft, propelled by sail and long sweeps. The spring tide was already flowing, lacking but two hours to high water at our *rendez-vous* point, and the dark current of the Saguenay met the dancing sunlit water of the St. Lawrence with swirls and eddies. Whoever was at the wheel had his hands full as we altered course to port and approached our goal.

The fires were banked and the steam gauges were up to the mark, and I had taken the moment to poke my head out of the after hatch again, braving the possible wrath of Jean-Baptiste. I wished I had my service binoculars with which to scan the horizon to the east. For if the royal yacht were to keep its *rendez-vous* deep within the fiord of the Saguenay, it was not unlikely that its masts were about to appear over the rim of the ocean. No sooner had I formed the thought than the commander appeared from below. He stood erect in the conning tower, stretching to his full height in an attempt to extend his view of the horizon from the low-lying decks of our vessel, a scant few feet above the ocean's surface. He wedged himself against the slight roll of the submersible, put his binoculars to his eyes, and commenced to sweep the empty waters. Minutes passed before he concentrated at last on one spot on the distant horizon, adjusting his glasses slightly.

I could almost feel his reaction to the moment. Through the glasses, the waves of the sea would be foreshortened. The horizon would appear not as a straight ruled line, but as a tumble of glistening water in which the senses could be deceived. The masts of a ship "hull down" could poke briefly above the gleaming billows, then as quickly disappear, and one could be left with a sense almost of hallucination, until, if the vessel were approaching, the topmasts would again heave into the distant view and confirm their reality.

It is my belief, based on my experience on the Afghan frontier, in the South Seas, and at home in the curious underworld that is the England of Sherlock Holmes, that a man experiences the greatest sense of elation and well-being not after a good meal, or in the arms of a loving woman, but in the face of risk and challenge. I have felt such sensations with Holmes, cramped, cold, waiting in some dank and gloomy cellar for the arrival of an unknown adversary, and on the dark fogbound moors of Devonshire awaiting God knew what hound of hell. Even waiting for shot and shell on the Afghan frontier, one finds oneself absurdly singing snatches of song, joking, eyes bright, nerved up and ready. Then, abruptly, the action is joined, and every fibre of one's being is set on the task, however horrendous its execution may be. One is then so concentrated, so involved, one is in a kind of ecstacy, truly alive. Perhaps it is the experience, the promise of this strange transport of emotion that deludes man and calls him constantly to war, despite his reason and his knowledge that in the next moment he himself may be blown, shapeless, into Eternity, a torn carcass in the mud of the battlefield, or a lifeless form spiralling slowly into the unknown depths of the sea.

The sound of a bosun's pipe shrilled through the vessel. The word was passed: "Prepare to dive!" Two men I had not seen before — clearly electrical artificers — moved silently in rubber-soled shoes to their stations, as Louis Frechette and the other fireman went through an obviously well rehearsed procedure of closing down the steam engine and switching over to the accumulators. Suddenly the vessel was silent as a fish. Under electrical power, there was now a quiet hum instead of the familiar thump of the engines.

I was called to the wheel. The hatches had been closed and made watertight, and I had to go through the body of the submersible to get to my station. The two artificers were standing by a grey-painted steel bulkhead upon which a number of polished bronze wheels gleamed in the flickering overhead electric light. I saw a system of levers and gauges, connecting pipes, wires and switches. The Baron's voice came hollowly through the brass voice-pipe from the conning tower.

"Flood chambers two and three."

The older of the two artificers repeated the command, the bronze wheels were spun, and silently the submersible tilted forward at a slight angle and settled deeper in the water. I gained my post presently, and took over the wheel from a taciturn fellow who at once went below, presumably to another station. The Baron was conning the vessel himself, manipulating levers which controlled the angle of the hydroplanes like the lateral fins of a fish and steered the craft vertically to greater or lesser depths.

In a moment we were gliding effortlessly, totally submerged. The Baron's hands on the hydroplane controls were steady, holding the ship on a gentle forward incline. A pressure gauge showed our increasing depth. At twenty feet the sunlight still came to us, filtered through the water. At thirty, it was dim. At forty feet, when a glimmer of light still came from above, the Baron eased the controls and the ship levelled off. There was pressure in my ears, and the temperature in the confined space had perceptibly increased. I could understand submerging to escape detection, but why he chose to go so deep, I did not understand, unless it was simple curiosity.

The submersible had an optical device through which the commander could view, in a limited way, the passage ahead. It was a vertical tube, with its optical axis twice bent through a right angle by reflecting prisms and mirrors. But below a depth of twelve feet, this too was submerged, all visual contact with the outer world was broken, and we proceeded blind in an alien world. The Baron checked his timepiece.

"What is your course, Irishman?"

"Northwest by north, sir."

"Keep it there."

"Aye aye."

For the better part of an hour, we proceeded in a silence broken only by the hum of electric dynamos and the smooth passage of water past our cigar-shaped hull. The Baron had moved to a small chart table, where he took up a pair of dividers and busied himself measuring nautical distances. I could not help admiring the cool, professional manner with which he undertook his command, and I had to remind myself that he was in fact a cold-blooded killer bent on the destruction of our beloved Empire.

I considered grappling with him, seizing the hydroplane's levers, and plunging us wildly out of control into the dark depths of Saguenay's waters. Before I could make a decision about such a mad plan, he broke into my fevered thoughts.

"The chart reads 250 fathoms."

"Sorr?"

"We've got about a quarter of mile of water under us."

"Deep, sorr."

"It is indeed."

He continued with his calculations. I looked at his back, broad but vulnerable as he bent in concentration over the dimly lit chart table. In scant minutes, the deliberate actions of this man would take the life of the future King, in a conflagration that could ignite the world.

My course was clear. I would make a sudden leap, heart pounding in a red-misted courage born of desperation. Mad grappling in mortal combat, control levers thrust awry, would plunge us mutually twisting to our death in the abyss. My heart was in my throat.

Quietly, gently to himself, the Baron was singing. I felt the hairs rise on my neck, it contrasted so with my rage!

"'Tis the rising of the moon, 'tis the rising of the moon, and hurrah me boys for freedom, 'tis the rising of the moon. Hurrah me boys for freedom!" he sang. He finished his precise calculations, straightened up, turned, and caught my eye with a grin. "Irishman, we're about there. We'll go up and take a look. Hold your course."

"Aye, aye, sorr," said I.

Gone was the moment of action, or I had not been man enough to take it. He ascended again to his perch, and addressed a voice pipe. "Ballast tanks two and three. Prepare to blow."

Hollow responses came over the voice pipe from the ballast control positions.

"Blow ballast tanks two and three."

A pump started somewhere. The Baron adjusted the hydroplane controls, and the boat tilted up gently by the bows. The pressure gauge marked our ascent. At ten feet below the surface we levelled off while the Baron peered through his omniscope, as the optical tube was called.

Suddenly he swore an oath in German.

"Hard a-port!" he roared.

Without thought I swung the wheel. "Hard a-port!" I cried.

The craft answered the helm, coming around quite smartly for a vessel of her proportions. I looked up at the Baron. His face was distorted with rage and anguish. The conning tower broke water and sunlight flared through the streaming port holes.

"Stop engines!" roared the Baron into the voice pipe. A bell rang below.

"Engines stopped, sir."

"Full astern!"

"Full astern." The bell rang, and the ship shuddered as her motive power was reversed.

"Midships!"

I spun the wheel blindly.

There was a jarring crash as our ship, eighty tons of metal, engines, boilers, torpedoes, still moving slowly ahead, collided broadside with a solid object I could not at the moment see. Only the Baron was able to discern what was happening on the surface, and he surely did not like it.

"Stop engines!"

I verily believe that had the Baron and I been on the same side we could have salvaged a tricky situation. Because of his quick responses we had avoided running full tilt into one of the log rafts that infest these waters. As it was, we had struck a glancing blow only, and were still navigable. We could have submerged and gone on our way, leaving yet another legend about some "monster of the deep" to be told around the winter fires.

But Fate and Sherlock Holmes deemed it otherwise. The raft was one of those that are commonplace on the rivers, drifting to their destinations with the current, under makeshift sails and formidable sweeps manipulated by eight or ten men, who in their off hours take shelter in small shanties built directly on the great logs. Distorted through the west glass of the ports of the conning tower, such a group faced us now. As the submersible swung around, answering the helm, I saw through the streaming glass that, dressed in rough mackinaws, their bright tuques and sashes and their heavy spiked logging boots, a dozen of these swarthy fellows stood on the heaving logs, sharp-pointed pike poles at the ready, watching us.

The submersible, all way taken off her, came to rest alongside the raft. The men on the logs hooked their pike poles to keep her there. The Baron spoke sharply into the voice pipe.

"All hands remain at your stations. Jean-Baptiste, report to the wheelhouse."

In a moment the fellow pushed his way up past an anxious-faced artificer and joined us in the limited space.

"M'sieur?"

"Jean-Baptiste, I am going to open the hatch. You speak to these men. Tell them we are on secret manoeuvers for the freedom of Quebec. They will understand you."

"*Oui*, m'sieur le Baron."

Jean-Baptiste pushed past us and released the holding-down bolts that secured the watertight hatch. Fresh air, like the breath of heaven, flowed in. I could hear bird song, the sounds of water, and hoarse male voices from the occupants of the raft. Also, faintly, absurdly, I could hear the sound of music: a military band was playing the overture to *Iolanthe*. I shook my head in disbelief.

The raft and the submersible together had swung with the current of the river, so that the Baron and I saw the source of the music at the same moment. Coming towards us up the river, still half a mile distant, shining, gleaming in the sun, its band playing, was Her Majesty's yacht *Victoria and Albert*. She must have seen the great log raft ahead, obstructing the channel, for she gave a single blast on her whistle and altered course to starboard, proceeding parallel to the ancient cliffs, half a mile away, which reached two thousand feet into the sky. There was no human habitation to be seen in the desolation of this remote place — truly, as the Indians said, the abode of evil spirits. The sound of the ship's whistle reverberated from cliff and crag in ever diminishing echoes, the band played on, and whether those in the royal yacht had in fact seen the submersible lying in wait, low in the water beside the log raft, I could not tell.

The alteration of her course brought the *Victoria and Albert* around to such an angle that instead of being bows on to us as before, she now presented us with a broader view, almost the whole length of the vessel. On his perch in the conning tower I felt the Baron tense and shift position, watching and waiting. He crouched a little, peering down the length of the submersible's foredeck. I saw that at her present course and speed, the royal yacht would cross our bows less than a quarter of a mile distant, well within range of the Whitehead torpedoes with which we were equipped. The long foredeck, from the Baron's point of view, was like a gun sight pointing two deadly charges at their target.

"Set both torpedoes to fire," said the Baron quietly into the voice pipe. A moment elapsed, then back came the hollow response: "Both torpedoes set to fire."

The calculations that would go through the Baron's brain at that moment were likely almost automatic. Anyone who has shot game birds in flight, and most European gentry have done so, by that exercise has become skilled in the science of ballistics, at least in the judgment of "aim off" — the relative time of flight between bullet and target. Rate of Change of Range, it is termed in the Navy *Gunnery Manual*. I could feel the Baron waiting for the exact moment for his shot.

On the raft, a fight had broken out. A burly *bucheron* had challenged Jean-Baptiste, and on the slippery surface of the logs they were facing each other with grasping hands and flailing spiked boots. The *Victoria and Albert* continued to bear down, band playing, all unknowing.

The Baron on his perch stood between me and the open hatchway. He must have trusted me, for I am sure I took him by surprise, charging into him as if in a rugger scrum. But like a rock he stood his ground, legs braced, eye steady. He pressed the switch that released one torpedo. A moment later, as he released the other, there was a sibilant hiss of compressed air being vented, and at the bows of the vessel spray was thrown up as the deadly Whitehead torpedoes plunged into the water and headed for their target. The release of the torpedoes' weight brought the nose of the submersible up out of the water with a lurch that destabilized her, so that she settled perceptibly by the stern. At the same moment, like a wounded tiger, the Baron leaped upon me. Caught off balance, I went down, his hands on my throat.

In the confined space I vainly sought to break the Baron's steely grip. We tumbled to the cold, metal deck of the wheel house. He was on top of me, blocking out the heavenly blue of the sky, and I could not effectively seize him to break his hold. I struggled and kicked, and grasping his wrists endeavoured to claw his fingers from my windpipe. I felt my senses going.

Then there was a sudden, shattering explosion close at hand, an eruption which reverberated through the vessel's hull with the resonance of a great bell being struck. Miraculously, the Baron's awful hold was broken. I gasped for air and the darkness lifted. Above me now stood Louis Frechette, a short iron winch-bar in his hand. On the deck beside me lay the limp body of the Baron.

A second explosion rocked our vessel. With scant ceremony, Frechette pulled me to my feet and shoved me up and out the hatch into the purity of daylight. As I emerged into the open air, with dazed eyes I saw, sweeping towards me across the black surface of the river, a smooth solid wall of water. Without foam or ripple it came, increasing in size, moving silently like an evil emanation from the deep.

Beyond it, the *Victoria and Albert* was coming around in a tight circle. Between us was a steam launch, sparks flying from its smokestack, as it manoeuvered amidst a sea of logs.

I turned my attention back to the oncoming mass of dark water. Like a monstrous living thing it reached the raft and lifted it bodily, sending the makeshift shanties flying and forcing its occupants to scramble and hang on for dear life. On the lee side of the vessel, I made an attempt to reach the raft, but was myself engulfed. The evil current overflowed the submersible, flooding in through the newly opened hatches, shifting the vessel's critical balance of buoyancy, flowing into its inner recesses.

Despairing, but thinking I might somehow reach the raft, I jumped into the water. With an immense sigh the submarine slowly turned over on its side and sank, and I was dragged down with the doomed vessel into the cold depths of that Stygian stream. I struggled, with bursting lungs, fearful that in the frigid water the submarine's super-heated boilers would burst. Then somehow my mind became curiously clear: the boilers would not explode, for they had been closed down for over an hour, and must have cooled off. I felt deliriously pleased with myself.

A sudden gout of released air from the sinking vessel caught and propelled me to the surface. The turbulence flung me up under the log raft, where I struck my head and sank again. A second time I rose, this time alongside the logs, to see the precious blue sky and to gulp some air into my tortured lungs. I was conscious of figures on the raft, rough words in *joual*, heavy caulked boots, willing hands reaching out to assist me to safety. I saw a beak-nosed Indian with long and sinewy arms, and a fellow with flaming red hair whose missing hand had been replaced with a hook. I saw François Leblanc, rising bloodily from the prone insensible figure of that miscreant Jean-Baptiste.

And I glimpsed the Union Jack floating from the topmast of a trim steamship, and a ship's boat proceeding at a smart pace towards us.

# Chapter XVI
# A Demonstration
# aboard the Yacht

I awakened to find Sherlock Holmes bending over me, his grey eyes full of concern. For any contrary impression I may have given elsewhere, I apologize: Holmes is not entirely successful in his pose as a cold, precise, calculating machine devoid of human emotion, and on this occasion I suppose I had earned a moment of affection from him.

"Hullo, old friend," he said. "I'm sorry I arrived a bit late."

"It's all right," I replied groggily, trying to sit up. "Where am I?"

"Aboard the steam yacht *Victoria and Albert*. Here, try some chicken broth." He reached a long arm for a silver tureen. "It has in it a dash of excellent sherry. Compliments of the Prince's chef."

Gratefully I sipped the hot mixture, and as warmth flowed into me I became conscious of my surroundings. Dressed in pale blue silk pajamas, I lay in embroidered satin sheets amongst feather pillows. Behind Holmes, a beam of sunlight glinted off the burnished brass of a cabin porthole. The tureen from which he had spooned the hot broth was engraved with the feathers of the Prince of Wales.

"He is very pleased," said Holmes.

"Who?" I asked, stupidly.

"His Royal Highness, the Prince of Wales," said Sherlock Holmes.

"Oh," I said. "That's nice." And I fell into a deep slumber.


I do not know how far His Royal Highness's incognito visit to the dark waters of the Saguenay was publicized, or how much hunting of moose, bear and wildfowl this keen sportsman and his party were able to enjoy before, loaded with trophies, they turned the yacht's slender bow again towards Britain. Mycroft had used the word "hunting," but the Prince may have done no hunting at all in the usual sense.

I did attend a modest ceremony on the open ship's deck, where I was presented to the Prince along with the ebullient Hiram Maxim, reunited at last with his beautiful consort, Madeleine de

Vernisse. A sleek Indian canoe lay cradled on deck alongside the ship's longboat, attesting to the manner in which Maxim and his lady had intercepted the royal yacht after a headlong flight, night and day, down the rushing waters of the St. Lawrence.

Holmes, in his turn, had recruited Louis Leblanc, the brother of the mourned Philomel, taking the steam launch from the shipyards in Quebec to *rendez-vous* with a team of raftsmen in the Saguenay, barely in time to provide a screen of log rafts for the protection of the Royal vessel. It was against this screen that the Baron's surface torpedoes had exploded, so close to the submersible that through her open hatches she was flooded and sent to the bottom.

To the shrill sound of the bosun's pipe, the Prince of Wales welcomed us on the open deck of the *Victoria and Albert*. He was shorter than I had remembered, but made up for his lack of stature by his regal bearing. He affected a trim brown beard, and a peaked officer's cap bearing the insignia of the Royal Yacht Squadron. His royally corpulent figure was encased in a brass-bound Navy reefer jacket.

"A most impressive performance, Monsieur Maxim," he said. "What there was of it."

"It was a gamble, Your Royal Highness."

"Gambling is a vice — "

"Sire?"

"When done for stakes people cannot afford."

The Prince of Wales chuckled at his own *bon mot*, and from his entourage came a polite ripple of laughter.

"Well, sir, I'm real sorry it sank before you got a good look at it. I had intended to show off its remarkable capabilities on the surface and underwater, speed, manoeuverability — streets ahead of the Nordenfeldt, may I say!"

"Otherwise, His Royal Highness would not be here," admonished a senior aide-de-camp.

"Sorry, sir, of course," said Maxim. "I sure do appreciate that. It's just that I figure the way things are shaping up with the French, and the Germans, and the Russians, the British Navy could do with a few submarines for defense purposes."

"If you'll permit me, sire?" A red-faced Admiral spoke up, his wardroom accent in wondrous contrast to Maxim's American tones.

"Yes, Tuggy," replied the Prince.

"I wish to go on record that I believe the Royal Navy is not in need of protection, and that Monsieur Maxim's submersible boat is underhand, unfair, and damned un-English!"

"Really, Tuggy?"

"It is the weapon of an inferior power, and Britain, being a superior power, does not need it."

"Thank you, Tuggy. We shall note your remarks," said the Prince. "And now, if the ladies will forgive our concern for weapons of war, we have a surprise of our own for Monsieur Maxim."

He made a slight gesture with his hand, and at once a bright young gunnery officer with shiny gaiters stepped smartly forward, accompanied by two ratings. He saluted and proceeded at the double with his small party to the foredeck, where on a slightly raised platform, on command, they removed a fitted, brilliantly white canvas cover, and revealed to our sight the M-gun itself.

"Good God, sir!" exclaimed Maxim. "My gun!"

"Your gun, indeed, Maxim. We propose a small demonstration."

"Your Royal Highness is gracious."

The Prince motioned again, and an equerry stepped forward, bearing a pair of binoculars on a cushion. He took the glasses up and, adjusting them to his sight, scanned the surface of the river. The members of the Royal entourage waited, silently watching, as the gunnery team stood by the gleaming weapon, ready to fire, awaiting Royal instruction.

"Target bearing left!" cried the Prince.

The M-gun swivelled smoothly to port. A great pine tree was floating half-submerged some five hundred yards distant from the ship. "Target on, sir," cried the gunnery officer.

"Open fire!"

The M-gun burst into life, and its snake-like belt of ammunition threaded without hesitation through the firing mechanism. As the water around the floating log erupted in foam, the tree itself was riddled, smashed, and splintered with the concentrated rain of .303 Martin-Henry cartridges descending upon it. From the looming cliffs across the dark water, echoes from the gun's firing were multiplied a thousandfold.

The Prince raised his hand, and the firing ceased. So, too, did the echoes, sounding further and further away, until all was silent. From the Royal entourage came a sedate ripple of applause.

"M-gun secure, sir!" piped up the young gunnery officer in his shiny gaiters.

"Very good," responded our Royal host.

"That is amazing, sir, if I may say so," commented Hiram Maxim.

"Why do you say so?"

"When I had the privilege of displaying the weapon in London, I was real embarrassed. Black powder clogged up the mechanism, and it packed up in short order. From what I have just seen, it seems to work perfectly!"

"Let us just say, Monsieur Maxim, to use your colourful phrase, we got the bugs out!"

The Prince favoured my friend Sherlock Holmes with a look and a quiet nod. Holmes, now soberly dressed as an aide-de-camp, was inconspicuous amongst the Royal entourage. I saw him incline his head in silent acknowledgement of the compliment to his expertise.

"We see a future for that weapon in the defence of the Empire," said the Prince to Hiram Maxim.

The purpose of Holmes's activity in the laboratories of Montpellier was now transparent — the goal of what he had described as research into the "coal-tar derivatives." He was in fact developing a smokeless high explosive for a specific purpose while he was presumed to have perished in the frightful cauldron below the Reichenbach Falls. Only his highly placed brother Mycroft had been privy to his secret.

I saw that the pursuit of Baron von Kramm and the plan to acquire the M-gun for British use had begun much sooner than I had presumed. Holmes obviously had certain facts at his fingertips by the time he turned up in my rooms in London. "We shall be in the same boat," he had said. Maxim's passage to Quebec had been booked long before I knew that Holmes was alive, and in fact before he had made his public threat to remove the gun from England.

As for the Baron, that classic *agent provocateur*, how long, I wondered, had he known of the capabilities of Maxim's fearsome gun? On whose orders was he prepared to assassinate the future King, an action that would, had Holmes not forestalled it, have roused disastrous echoes around the world?

Nor could I tell exactly what role the beautiful Madeleine de Vernisse had played in these strange events. Even my own attempt to take over the reins of my life by going abroad as a ship's surgeon had evidently been used, without my knowledge, as a move in someone else's game.

"We are all pawns, Watson, in games we cannot begin to understand," Holmes had said. I had much to ask him when the opportunity arose, though I could not tell what questions he would be prepared to answer.

Wearily, I took a deep breath of the pure air, scented with the pine and spruce of that unspoiled Canadian wilderness.

The decor of the ornate Grand Cabin of the *Victoria and Albert* was more appropriate to a reception room in the court of St. James than to a seagoing vessel. In this grandiose setting, Madeleine de Vernisse was formally presented by an aide-de-camp to the Prince. Holmes and I were invited to attend.

It would appear that the Prince and the lady were not absolute strangers. As she had stated earlier to Holmes, in her travels on the Continent and her very successful performances in the capitals of Europe, she had occasion to meet powerful, important, and influential people. The Prince himself was a patron of music, who loved the delights of France, and those of Paris in particular, being a welcome guest as much in the theatres and concert salons as in the great houses of the nobility. Undoubtedly, their paths had crossed.

Now, he courteously took the lady's dainty hand in his, held it for a moment, and raised it to his lips. Then, upon a gesture from the Prince, an equerry stepped forward with a flat case, covered in fine old red morocco leather. This he handed to the Prince, who, turning to Madame de Vernisse, snapped open the lid. Revealed inside, cradled in worn red velvet, were two beautifully-crafted French duelling pistols of the time of Louis XIV.

"These, madame, belong in your family, we believe. And it gives us great pleasure, after a hundred years, to return them to you."

Her eyes darkened with emotion. "Yes, Your Royal Highness, I had heard of the pistols."

"They are yours, madame."

"May I handle them?"

"They are yours to do with as you wish."

In my mind's eye, I was again in the Château de Vernisse, viewing the hundred-year-old portrait of the beautiful Amalie. I recalled Madeleine's voice, "My grandmother. . . . It was painted when Edward, Duke of Kent, lived here. He was the father of your Queen Victoria." Clearly depicted in that painting were these identical pistols, one in its nest of red velvet, the other firmly grasped in Amalie's right hand.

What stormy scenes of love and passion had these weapons witnessed? What affairs of honour had been at stake; what affairs of the heart? I had the feeling of intruding on private matters of the utmost delicacy, as the grandson of the Duke of Kent returned the pistols to the granddaughter of Amalie.

A moment passed; then, as if she were striking a quiet chord of music, the lady's slender fingers descended upon the ancient pistols. She took each in turn from its velvet cradle, and bent her lovely head to examine the fine silver-work on butt and barrel.

". . . in the full bloom of arrogant young manhood . . ."

Presently she selected one of them and weighed it in the palm of her hand. Her fingers closed around it in a decisive grip. Her head came up, and she glanced around the Royal cabin as if seeking a target. Bertie watched her with a quiet smile. Affixed to the panelling was more than one painting of distinction. Our gracious Queen Victoria was represented, as were the late Prince Consort and other members of the Royal Family. Madame de Vernisse turned away from the Prince and found her target. Raising the pistol at arm's length, she sighted down the length of the royal suite. On the far bulkhead, held in her unwavering aim, was a full-length portrait of Edward, Duke of Kent, father of Queen Victoria, in the full bloom of arrogant young manhood. Lean and handsome, in a pose full of authority, military cocked hat worn at a dashing angle, he was dressed in his regalia as Colonel of the Royal Fusiliers of Quebec. A senior aide-de-camp made a movement towards Madame de Vernisse, but the Prince raised his finger and stayed the man's intervention.

What secret anguish Madeleine was assuaging, I could only surmise. Had the pistol been loaded, I am not sure where the impetuous spirit of this woman would have led. Presently, she lowered the weapon again, and cradled it close to her. She turned to Holmes and myself.

"*Regardez*, messieurs," she said in low tones.

I looked where she indicated. The butt of each pistol was engraved with a facsimile of the Golden Dog, crouched forever, gnawing his bone. Around the base of each, was a line of poetry in old French. She read it aloud, in a low voice: "*Un temps viendra qui n'est pas venu, Que je mordrai qui m'aura mordu.*"

Madeleine de Vernisse looked up, her dark eyes directly upon the Prince. In response, he smiled at her gently.

"*Ah oui, madame, mais qui n'est pas venu*," he said.

"*Mais, un temps viendra*, Your Royal Highness," she replied, "a time will come."


There is little more to add to the story. Madeleine de Vernisse elected to return to her château on the heights of the Citadel of Quebec, with her music, her memoirs, her emeralds and her pistols. Hiram Maxim returned in the royal yacht to England, where he took out British citizenship, and was knighted by Queen Victoria. In due course he was able to demonstrate his theory of heavier-than-air flight. His machine gun was manufactured in sufficient quantity to supply every battalion in the British Army in time for the Boer War, and Her Majesty's Government ordered a trial lot of submarines, five of them to begin with, to be built by Vickers &

Son and Maxim, in association with the Electric Boat Company of New York.

The Baron von Kramm was drowned in the sinking of Maxim's submersible in the Saguenay River, or so I have some reason to believe.

As for myself, I sought a quieter life for a time in Ontario, near Niagara Falls, where a nephew of mine was about to acquire what was advertised as a fine estate complete with manor house, and well trained servants in the best of English county tradition. I thought I might visit him for a bit.

I met Bloody Red O'Connell, now a raftsman, and thanked him for helping to rescue me from the Saguenay.

"Och, it was the hook that pulled yez out of the water, sorr. The thanks be to yourself, entoirely!"

I never learned, for sure, what it was that shattered his arm, or whether he was in any way connected with the dark purpose of the Fenians.

And what of my friend Holmes? Officially he was dead — lying lifeless somewhere in the awful chasm of the Reichenbach Falls — and he elected to remain that way for a time, taking the opportunity to enjoy some private life. There were so many things he wanted to pursue. He wanted to track down a creature known as the "Windigo," a frightful thing of the Northern woods, feared by the Indians, a monster with burning eyes and a heart of ice, whose very appearance drove mad those venturing too far into the wilderness. He was also fascinated by the maps of Quebec and Ontario, poring over them with his magnifying lens.

"Meteorites."

"What?"

"Those lakes in the far north. Perfectly circular, formed by small meteorites coming in from outer space with tremendous force, generating immense heat and pressure."

"Yes, I suppose so."

"Watson, do you not see how suggestive that is?"

"No, I'm afraid I don't follow you, Holmes."

"When immense heat and pressure are applied to carbon, what is the result?"

"I believe that is how diamonds are created."

"Exactly!" cried Holmes, rubbing his hands together in excitement. "Now, suppose there are coal fields in that area." He jabbed at the map with a long forefinger.

"Yes?"

"What is coal, other than a form of carbon?"

"Holmes," I said, the light beginning to dawn, "Can you possibly mean — "

"I mean it is not outside the bounds of possibility that there may be, awaiting our discovery, diamonds of a size undreamed-of!"

But before Holmes could pursue further his own adventures, he was obliged to go to Montreal and Ottawa on certain matters of State which I am not at liberty to divulge, having perhaps said too much already. After that he proposed to return to Quebec for a time, to continue his music studies under the guidance of none other than Madame de Vernisse. She had observed that it would be a pity if her priceless Stradivarius fell into disuse, for lack of anyone to play it.

Other Sherlockian titles from Simon & Pierre

*In Bed with Sherlock Holmes, Sexual Elements in Arthur Conan Doyle's Stories of the Great Detective*, by Christopher Redmond
ISBN 0-88924-142-2  6 x 9, 208 pages, illustrated, 1984


*Welcome to America, Mr. Sherlock Holmes, Victorian America meets Arthur Conan Doyle*, by Christopher Redmond
ISBN 0-88924-184-8  6 x 9, 236 pages, map, 1987


*The Sherlock Holmes ABC Book, An Illustrated Introduction to the Great Detective*, by Andy and Bill Paton
ISBN 0-88924-155-4  6 x 9, 64 pages, illustrated, 1985